PRAISE FOR THAT VERY PLACE

McGuigan masterfully explores the tender space between connection and estrangement, the cost of words unspoken, and the reverberating legacy of parents who abandon and abuse their children and the children who turn away. McGuigan's prose is unflinching, precise and dreamlike.

—Sonja Livingston, author of *Ghostbread*

That Very Place features a cast of strong women who carry painful regrets, dream of futures just beyond their grasps, and find grace in the smallest things. To read a McGuigan story is to feel the truth of what one character says toward the end of this collection: "Family's a complicated business." McGuigan has a keen eye for the compromises and accommodations we make when duty collides with yearning. These are glorious stories.

—Lee Martin, author of the Pulitzer Prize Finalist, *The Bright Forever*

McGuigan's stories deftly address dangerous and difficult subjects—physical and emotional abuse, parental abandonment, dementia—all without even a whiff of melodrama. Her characters are utterly compelling and so complex that sometimes they are unwittingly complicit in the traumas inflicted on them and on the people they most love and try to protect. The collection is a deeply moving descent into the human heart and all of its conflicts, mysteries, failures, and triumphs.

    —David Jauss, author of *Glossolalia: New & Selected Stories*

In *That Very Place*, Mary Ann McGuigan brings to life vivid, unforgettable characters, each facing unexpected upheaval. McGuigan's stories deftly capture life's unpredictability, and the simple truth that how we face our troubles determines who we are. Written with compassion and skill, these stories are filled with honesty, sensitivity, and ultimately hope.

    —Dinty W. Moore, author of *The Mindful Writer*

THAT VERY PLACE

Stories

Mary Ann McGuigan

Also by Mary Ann McGuigan

Pieces: A Novel in Stories
Crossing Into Brooklyn
Morning in a Different Place
Where You Belong
Cloud Dancer

ACKNOWLEDGMENTS

"Because Her Hour Is Come" (*The Massachusetts Review*, Fall 2022)

"Beloved" (*Prime Number Magazine*, October 1, 2016; reprinted in *Fresh.ink* September 13, 2021)

"The Beginner" (As "Tiny Dancer" in *Youth Imagination*, Silver Pen, May 2016; reprinted in *Random Sample*, July 29, 2022)

"The Broken Place" (*Cortland Review*, November 1, 2015; reprinted in *Fragmented Voices*, Dec. 17, 2021)

"The Sorrow for Her Loss" (*Stygian Lepus*, May 2023)

"Here and Now" (as "A Brutal Place" in *Fine Lines*, June/July 2023)

"Everything Nice" (as "Rites of Passage" in Invisible City, March 4, 2024

"The Last of the Darlin' Boys" (Halfway Down the Stairs, June 1, 2024)

To my writing buddies from VCFA and elsewhere who read these stories and were kind enough not to recommend I try binge watching instead.

To all those similarly addicted—whether to words or something even worse.

To Patrick and Douglas, who've shown me yet again that this writing stuff isn't really so important.

STORIES

THAT VERY PLACE

BELOVED

The windows in the rear of the Laundromat were open, but the June breeze that lifted the white wedding bunting tacked to the frames cooled no one, not even the ceiling flies. The place smelled like cheap cologne, the kind Walmart sells by the quart, and Maria figured at least a pint of it had been let free in the room. But it couldn't camouflage the odors that ruled here, fabric softener, detergent, bleach. About a dozen other customers, most clustered near the entrance in case some cool air found its way in, stood wiping brows and folding clothes into baskets. Coarse laughter drifted in from the street, where the groom's ushers, in their dark gray tuxedos with silky lapels, stood having a last-minute smoke.

Maria reached into the dryer, wanting to leave before the circus got underway, but her slacks—the only good pair that fit now—were still damp, and she had nothing else decent enough to wear to her meeting with the agency. She'd been given short notice, and with less than an hour left to get there, she had no time to buy something new. The first time she'd met with the family-placement agent, everyone in the room was wearing a suit, and Maria felt like a vagabond. Even her huge belly didn't seem like reason enough for jeans.

A week ago, the happy mother in the next bed—one of those bright bubbly types who made her wish they'd ban strollers from parks—had assured her that nursing would flatten her tummy. No help there. She sat down on one of the orange plastic chairs near the dryers and tried not to think about what she'd wear every day when she returned to work or how she'd dodge questions about life as a new parent, because she'd made up her mind not to be one, not by herself.

Mrs. Ortez, the mother of the bride, a small woman in a dress with a plunging neckline and too many lavender sequins, stepped daintily over the spots of soapy water that dotted the concrete floor. Her long taffeta skirt stirred up stray balls of the multicolored lint that materialized out of nowhere. From the shelf that ran the length of the wall someone had hung a sign: *Congradulations Rosa and Ricky.* Mrs. Ortez pointed to it proudly. Her two youngest had made it, she explained, as if someone had asked. One or two of the customers seated beneath the words nodded politely as they waited for socks and shirts to stop spinning.

According to Rosa, it had taken almost three months to get her mother to agree to have the wedding in the Laundromat, but this was where she had met Ricky and where he had proposed. Maria saw Rosa here often, admired her flawless skin and her long dark lashes, and wondered at her capacity to go on talking without a breath. They'd become, if not friends, at least laundry buddies. They were both born in the neighborhood, although Maria had gotten her own place two years ago. As the wedding date came closer, Rosa insisted that Mayor Bloomberg would conduct the ceremony. Maria still found it hard to believe he'd show up. He'd married very few couples, but his term was ending and Ricky worked for the company the mayor owned, started in the mailroom right out of high school. The mayor had sworn Ricky to secrecy, but Maria doubted there was anyone left in the five boroughs who didn't know about it by now.

Rosa was no good at secrets. Waiting on a bench with Maria for towels to dry, she'd chatter away. Life for her was one long Christmas Eve, and she loved talking about the joys that awaited her—her honeymoon in Puerto Rico, her four-poster bed, her wedded bliss, the brown-eyed children. Rosa could make rinse cycles last an eternity. But Maria would listen politely, without a trace of envy, because domestic prizes were never what she coveted. She and Raoul were moving toward something different, something better. Their orbit intersected with people able to have finer things, expect them even. They were breaking away from their parents' world, with its numbing prescriptions for what life should be.

Maria spotted Mrs. Ortez heading her way, so she busied herself with her phone to avoid eye contact. She'd never had occasion to speak to the woman, but she felt as if she knew her, because Rosa loved to talk about her family—even her father's fragile finances, how much she and Ricky wanted to help out. Earlier, when Mrs. Ortez had seen Maria come into the Laundromat—her first visit since the baby was born—the woman gestured from across the room, putting her hand against her own girdled tummy, beaming, eager to convey congratulations and approval. Maria only nodded, as if the assumption was correct.

Mrs. Ortez kept up a nervous chatter, telling one of the bridesmaids to turn up the volume on her daughter's iPod to combat the noise of the rasping machines. Socks and panties jumped in the little round windows and heavy buttons on jeans and fatigues snapped intermittently against the glass, but nothing could be done about that. The place was, after all, open for business.

From habit, Maria kept an eye on the entrance, though she knew it wasn't likely Raoul would be around. She'd seen him only once since she left the hospital, coming up from the subway. He asked if everything had gone well, as if she'd been away visiting an ailing relative, someone terminally ill, whose fate was certain. She had no intention of telling him that she still had almost a month to change her mind about giving up the baby. It was none of his business anymore.

When Raoul stopped calling every day, stopped sending daisies to her office on Fridays, she convinced herself he'd come around, didn't see the shift for what it was. A special project at work was going to require lots of hours. She believed him. He stopped coming over on Tuesday nights—their night for binging on old movies. The third time it happened, she called him. It was late, and she'd made the mistake of watching a romantic comedy. The happy ending came, of course, despite the odds. Swept up in it, like an evangelist, she called and told him how much she loved him. "I know," he whispered, his tongue thick with sleep. "I know." She didn't realize then what he meant, that love was a loose end he'd have to find a way to tie up.

Baskets of white carnations and chrysanthemums sat atop each of the washers in the center of the Laundromat, set back-to-back in two rows. The petals trembled as the machines chugged like steam engines, dribbling suds onto the speckled tiles. Only two were empty and quiet. Mrs. Ortez closed their lids and tossed away the makeshift signs that read *BROKE*.

The guests would be arriving soon, and, of course, the mayor.

Maria glanced at the small bulletin board, the spot where Rosa and Ricky had met. The board was normally a patchwork of yellowing business cards and torn slips of paper: scrawled requests for rides, rewards offered for lost dogs, ads from handymen. Today it bore a nine-by-twelve photo of the happy couple, taken at Coney Island, just after their engagement.

Maria had met Raoul here as well. Summer. An excuse, for him at least, to wear very little. The way he folded sheets was like a caress. He did not flirt, not in any way she had encountered before. He talked about classes he was taking.

"I thought about film school," he said. "NYU. But not for long."

"Directing?" She imagined him standing bare-chested in some desert location, barking orders through a megaphone, sexier than the leading man.

He nodded. "That's where the real action is." He laughed, but she heard no conceit in it, only the practical way he had of knowing what would work and what wouldn't. "I wised up once I saw how tough it is to make any inroads." She suspected there was more to it, and he saw that, adding, "The markets suit me fine. They have their own stories." He tucked a strand of her hair behind her ear, and the tingling went straight to her groin. Later, it would make her nervous when he told her she was beautiful. She'd never seen herself that way, but before long she believed he meant it, because his looks made women stare, and she doubted he'd have bothered with her if she wasn't a match.

She saw from the start that his ambitions were as big as her own, and she liked it that way. He was trading for Citigroup, the youngest guy on the floor. She'd been with Goldman Sachs for four years, moving to the trading floor only the year before. Their jobs were about risk, about the unknown, and she relished the mystery as much as he.

The machines hummed and wheezed, gurgled and gushed. As Mrs. Ortez passed each one, she centered the flowers once again. The vibrations had moved some of them perilously close to the edge. Maria thought of her own mother, of the comfort it would have been over the past several weeks to have a caring hand to steady her. Once the woman understood that Maria planned to give up the baby, their connection shriveled. Her mother's attempts to dissuade her didn't last. The shock of it made the woman lose her bearings; she had no frame of reference for such a choice.

Guests were entering now, wearing well-pressed suits and light gauzy dresses, Mrs. Ortez hurrying over to greet them, and Maria felt suddenly foolish, as if *her* reason for being there was the one that made no sense. She opened the dryer door again, saw Mrs. Ortez peeking at its contents. Something wasn't right. It held nothing pink or blue. Maria felt the urge to defend herself, as she had with Raoul, when she'd waited so long to tell him she was pregnant.

Her secrecy at first was part denial. Her breasts were tender, her period hadn't come, but no, it couldn't be. They'd been so careful.

Then denial gave way to defiance. So what if she was pregnant? It would be wonderful. They were so close by then, her books kicked under his bed, his clothes left hanging in her closet. They let themselves get lost in museums and the narrow streets downtown. She just wanted a little more time, to be sure that the way he held her, the way he sought her out when things went well meant he would understand that nothing they had would be spoiled. Their lives would change, yes, but that didn't have to be a bad thing.

When she finally told him, Raoul made a convincing case that it was. He was unfazed, believing she'd want their old routines to go unchanged—pricey red wine that made them sleep late on Saturdays, rainy Sundays with the *Times*, late-night talks about their work, their hopes of moving up. He assumed she'd want to be rid of it as well. Once he sensed the change in her, the desire, he began his retreat, like a man relieved he hadn't paid his deposit.

"It's a girl," she told him, well into her sixth month. She hadn't seen him in more than two weeks and didn't expect to find him in the Laundromat. She'd had the sonogram that day, and he hadn't answered her calls. She'd gone for the test by herself, the waiting room stocked with parenting magazines and women sure of what awaited them at home.

He leaned into the barrel of the washing machine and came up with one last sock, then straightened up to face her. "You're really going to do this?" he said. He sounded baffled, as if she'd made up her mind to try some daredevil stunt that had been done already, too many times before, something no one would pay to see.

"It's growing so fast," she said, convinced he didn't mean to sound so hurtful. "It's been kicking harder lately." She smiled, put her hand on her belly. She longed for him to do the same.

He didn't. He folded his towels—dark, outsized masculine things that managed to express what he left unspoken. He already had everything he needed.

She caught a glimpse of herself in a mirror behind him. The only frosted highlights left in her hair were at the tips, uneven and thin. She wished she had at least put on some mascara. Her face seemed swollen, unpleasantly ripe, like the rest of her. "I get four months of maternity leave. Paid," she said, desperate to make him see that the baby wouldn't be disruptive. He nodded but she could see that getting his luxurious towels into his laundry bag was the bigger concern. She told herself he would come around in the end. She had to, because it was too late to believe anything else.

The ordeal of it, the discomfort of the final trimester—the swollen legs, the pressure on her bladder—accelerated finally into pain that exploded from her lower back and gripped her torso. The spasms would recede, as if toying with her, and there were intervals when she dozed. The pain required all of her strength, but no resolve, because the goal would be accomplished with or without her consent. It was a climb up Mount Everest with no view, because by then she saw that the best thing, the prudent thing, was adoption. Without Raoul, she didn't want the baby.

When the child was born, Maria's first, absurd reaction was anger. She felt used by this new life. They cleaned the baby and brought her close, wearing a little pink cap. Maria touched the soft wool, but not the skin. The agency had gently discouraged Maria beforehand from nursing or naming the baby, and she didn't contest these limits. Still, she had feared, expected really, that once it was in her arms she would be drawn to the child, immediately attached. She felt nothing of the kind. It was a squirming, independent thing, fragile but sturdy, so present. It seemed unaware of her, ready to eat and cry and grow with or without Maria. It was helpless, but it didn't need her, not her especially, and though she wanted to feel essential, she understood that she wasn't. She felt no tenderness toward the child, no wish to keep it. She could move on without this creature. Nothing stirred in her. Her arms were so weak she feared the infant would slip from her grasp. The persistent pain and burning in her groin demanded her attention, and the relentless loneliness had not abated. No magic moment had come to take it away. It sat there, heavy on her chest, outweighing the lively bundle in her arms. This huge moment, like the others meant to mark a woman's life, had turned out to be a distraction, a milestone on a path that led nowhere. It was a lie.

She rang for the nurse, told her she could take the child away. Maria attempted a smile, but she saw it didn't fool the woman. As she handed her off, squirming and wiggling, she told the nurse she wanted them to change the baby's cap. She wanted a white cap for the girl. No uniform, no script.

Maria shifted in her orange chair, the plastic sticking to the backs of her thighs. The ushers had come in and were helping to find a chair or two for the older guests. People waiting for towels to dry happily gave up their seats. Maria relinquished hers to a middle-aged woman with a bottom so wide it spread regally beyond the chair's edges and made her silky dress ride up her thighs. Everyone seemed swept up now, attentive. Mayor Bloomberg was outside. The bride's limo was at the curb. Maria wasn't sure how she'd ever get out of the place. The entrance was blocked with serious men in dark suits and dark glasses, the mayor's people. She considered taking her pants, damp or not, and squeezing her way through, but Mrs. Ortez came running past, calling out, "The runner. We forgot the runner." Maria couldn't get by.

Lifting her swishing skirt, the woman hurried to the back wall where a bright roll of white plastic waited. She managed to tilt it onto the floor, but it was too heavy for her to unroll by herself. One of the ushers ran to help. Together they pulled the plastic between the line of washers and dryers as guests and customers parted and stood aside, like true believers, as if the runner offered a direction, not a dead end.

A breathless commotion by the doorway made people stand on their toes for a better view, and Maria found herself getting caught up in the promise. It filled the room like a herald's off-key trumpet. She had attended many weddings, and each one in its own way had been a study in self-absorption. People like Rosa saw nothing ahead but joyful possibilities, togetherness without guile.

The mayor, a short man wearing a precisely tailored suit from a pedigreed designer, stood at the entrance with his associates. One of them bent slightly to whisper something, pointing toward Mrs. Ortez. "Mayor Bloomberg," she cried. "This is so kind of you."

The mayor extended his hand. "Mrs. Ortez," he said. "Delighted."

"We're all ready for you," she said, never doubting he would come or that her daughter was anything but deserving of this departure from his schedule.

Bloomberg took in the room, deadpan. "I like what you've done with the place."

The laughter spread like a welcome breeze, then dutifully subsided as all heads turned to the bride standing with her father in the doorway, filmy silhouettes in the city sunlight. He was a stout, balding, tired-looking man, much like Maria's own father, with too many children and not enough resources. On his arm was a young woman Maria knew to be quite ordinary, about to marry an ordinary man. Yet everyone watching seemed transfixed, as if this event was remarkable enough to set aside their chores, to bear witness. Maria couldn't fight it off. She stretched to get a better look, saw the groom take Rosa's hand, the cuffs of his ill-fitting trousers already marked from the Laundromat floor. In their lilting Spanish accents, they repeated the words the mayor spoke with his slightly nasal twang. Customers dabbed tears away, and Maria's eyes burned as she thought of Raoul, of his strong grasp when he held her hand.

She turned her back to the drama, desperate to get out of there, and made her way to the dryer to check the pants. Dry, finally. By the time she folded them over her arm and found her jacket, the mayor was finishing up, moving toward the door with his people, haltingly stopping for the hands extended, returning the smiles. Rosa and Ricky followed a few steps behind, repeating their *thank you*s.

Maria was almost outside when she heard Mrs. Ortez calling to her. "Señora," she trilled, holding something out, as if it belonged to Maria, something she'd forgotten. She took it before she saw what it was—a newborn's tiny undershirt—then considered handing it back, explaining it wasn't hers, but the look of kinship on the woman's face wouldn't permit it.

Outside, the mayor's attendants hustled him into a big black car and the people gathering to watch blocked Maria's way to the trash container on the corner. So she tucked the shirt into the pocket of her jacket and hurried up the street. The material was impossibly soft, still warm, and she kept returning to it, secretly. It took no more than a stroke or two to imagine her nameless daughter bathed in harsh light, perhaps disturbed by the random little complaints of the other infants, waiting together, alone, the pale antiseptic place absorbing their novice sounds as if they were no more important than the hums and ticks of the room's intricate machinery.

The infant, unclaimed, would be too easy to disregard, and Maria feared for the child, felt a terrible connection, a fierce need to protect her. Panicky, she reached up and unfastened the tight clip from her hair, jerking her head from side to side, determined to shake off a feeling even more foolish than the baseless joy she'd witnessed in the Laundromat. She took longer, harder strides, enjoying how light she felt since the delivery, free again. But an absence registered now, a loss. She'd have to resist staking any foolish claims, fight the urge to be the one who decides for the girl.

No, not *the girl*. Elsa. She would think of her as Elsa, after her grandmother. What harm?

BECAUSE HER HOUR IS COME

She's sure she can't be dreaming, because she can feel Nora's hand on hers. The touch is light, barely there, but the cold bracelet is enough to bring her into the morning, back into the colorless room.

"Aunt Peggy," Nora whispers. "You're having a bad dream." The tips of Nora's fingers graze her forearm, but she pretends she's still asleep, because she wants it so badly, this contact. Nora rarely touches her anymore, not lovingly, so Peggy breathes her in, the coffee smell on her breath, the cologne that hints of sage and sea salt. It reminds her of the breeze off that lake near Derry, the one old Aunt Patsy insisted she visit, the one she swore could prevent a breech.

"Aunt Peggy, wake up," Nora says, touching her hand again. But Peggy doesn't have to open her eyes. She already knows what she'll see—the thick dark hair Nora thinks she got from her mother, the guarded blue eyes, more inscrutable each day. She'll be wearing a suit, something too conservative. She was promoted again last year, the prize for long hours and hard choices. Sometimes Peggy doesn't see her for days at a time.

Nora lets out a sigh, takes her hand away. Peggy suspects she's losing patience, eager to get Downtown. The whole business— looking after a sickly old woman, untangling the financial red tape— is clearly wearing on her. Visits are getting shorter and shorter, her willingness to listen, to be truly present, almost gone. So Peggy gives in, presses the sleep from her eyes.

"Your sisters again?" Nora says.

She nods, and Nora purses her lips as if Peggy brings the dreams on herself. But she's wrong. Peggy was the youngest, with no rank. Her sisters do as they please. Sometimes they appear in strong bodies, hair thick and dark and braided, shoes shined for a Sunday. Other nights they come in pain, skin loose and crepey on their arms, eyes filmy and defeated. Maureen, the oldest, the one who still has the last word, is always among them, unforgiving.

Lately her brothers are with them, figures without faces, but she knows it's them, laughing their brittle laughs, teasing the way they did when they were kids. Close up they smell like drink, like trouble. They talk as if they know where she is, what's happening to her, as if she's one of them now.

"Maybe it was that custard," Nora says. "You shouldn't eat right before bed." She strokes the hair at Peggy's temple, hesitant, as if she's touching a cat who might turn on her.

She's afraid, Peggy thinks. Or worse, repulsed. She prays it isn't that, prays Nora remembers she was attractive once, strong. "What a long list of *shouldn'ts* life is now," she mutters.

"No, no," Nora soothes, "everything's okay."

Peggy knows she doesn't believe that, because she's taken to stating the obvious—*Today is Saturday* or *You've already had your lunch*—as if the worst is already here. The sing-song tone makes plain her uncertainty about how much of what she says will get through. She doesn't share things anymore, come for advice the way she used to, worried about a new staffer or a stubborn client. Peggy always knew how to keep her from giving up on herself, on the way she wanted things to be. She was her role model growing up, her cheerleader when she reached the top.

The breakfast tray clanks and rattles its way into the room. Peggy doesn't have to look to know it's Carol, the one who never bothers to avoid disruption. As usual the toast smells burnt; it will be cold and soggy by the time it's buttered, the tea lukewarm. She eats very little these days, and hardly a bite when Carol serves.

Peggy sized her up early on: Less brains than a barnacle, this one, with the loose hems on her uniforms and her rough, stubby fingers. Peggy rarely speaks her name, and she's sure the woman has no clue why, and not the least concern. A person like Carol wouldn't have lasted a day on Peggy's staff. She treats her job the way she treats her appearance—with complete indifference.

Peggy won't let Carol wash her, not today. She can do it well enough on her own, though they all insist she can't. Let them insist all they want. She knows her temper can still clear a room.

Nora helps her sit up. "You're all right now?" She makes it sound like a question, when it isn't. Peggy knows there's only one answer she wants, so she tells her to run along, that she's fine. She doesn't mention the lapses anymore, the parts missing from the day. Sometimes she loses more than that. She loses her way altogether. The other day—it must have been early in the evening—she turned off the television and nothing in the room looked familiar. Nothing. Not one piece of the cheap, homogenized furniture, not even her photos. There were strangers in the frames. A woman standing in the doorway spoke her name but she didn't recognize her either. Someone else, with a voice as deep as a man's, led her to the bed, made her lie down.

Sometimes whole days are erased. She'll watch the rays of the morning sun slant into the room and the next thing she knows it's evening and Carol's face appears in the doorway, tinged with satisfaction, as if her suspicions are confirmed. Peggy feels time pushing at her then, poking a finger into her chest, like some uncompromising brute, insisting she give up her pointless attachments, accept that she's in charge of nothing anymore. The first woman to run a trading desk on Wall Street has no clout here, no purpose.

Nora steps away from the bed. "I'll come by tomorrow." She reaches for her handbag, and Peggy smiles for her.

"That would be good," she says. "There's something I'd like to talk with you about."

"What is it?" Nora's mouth tightens, the way it does when she thinks Peggy's about to intrude.

Peggy shrugs, as if it's nothing. "Just something I've been meaning to tell you."

Nora's gaze shifts to Carol, then back to Peggy. "Is everything all right here?" They've talked about the things that go on in nursing homes and Nora's on guard for the slightest misstep.

"Everything's fine here," Peggy says, as if that could ever be true. "It's just something I've had on my mind. For a long while."

Nora examines her face like a prosecutor, and Peggy wonders if it was a mistake to tell her even this much.

"It can wait," she says. "Go on before you're late."

"All right then. We'll talk tomorrow."

Peggy wonders if she'll kiss her cheek. She doesn't. She heads for the door, not even reluctantly.

She waits until Nora and Carol are gone before she tries the tea, though it hardly deserves the name. "The color of piss," her sister Bridget says. Bridget's voice is often in the room, all their voices, even when Peggy is certain she's awake. "How dare they call that tea?" Bridget says, ready as ever to fuss and complain. The lack of amenities in this place, no matter how expected—like this pitiful brew—still manages to annoy the hell out of Peggy. She's comforted that Bridget recognizes the insult, however routine it's become.

The greater insult is the room itself—boxy, inescapable. The colors of the walls and the chair and the bureau have faded, merged into a dismal, monotonous beige. Intended to be neutral, no doubt, brutally inoffensive.

She fights the sameness in her own small ways. Sometimes she rearranges the photos Nora hung on the walls, moves them from their assigned places. To the right of the window, there's an eight-by-ten of Peggy with her Analytics staff at the luncheon for her retirement. Even now she chuckles at how relieved they look. The photo of her parents is above the bureau, black and white, taken in the thirties. They're standing in front of a tall, iron gate that's been left ajar, and her father looks nervous, as if he's afraid he'll be expected to enter. His suit is dark, her dress gray with a white collar. She wears the same one in Peggy's dreams, although she invariably appears old, still in pain, ever the martyr, unwilling to accept life, especially everlasting.

The long wall opposite the bed has framed photos of Peggy with her sisters and brothers—on cruises, at baptisms and graduations— and several of her with the women from the parish, dear friends. She has stopped trying to remember their names. There are no pictures of her with Bill. That would only raise questions. The calendar is on the wall near the door, with May's sacred heart of Mary glowing in rays of pale blue and gold, but it's June now. She's sure of it.

She decides she'll scramble the photos again today, once she can get herself out of the damn bed. The first time she mixed them up, no one noticed, not even Louisa, whose vigilance is hawkish. Louisa's a kind bird, a worrier. She bothers to apply lotion after the wash. She speaks Peggy's name. She thinks she has secrets, but Peggy has guessed them. She's not supposed to be here. In that, they are alike. The woman is waiting for the authorities to discover this and send her home to a place she can barely remember. But Peggy has already been discovered, judged inept, without rights, banished from the life she knew. It was a shrinking life—she accepted that—but she had a kitchen, a mailbox, neighbors who knew her.

She's told Louisa about the dreams, how her sisters and brothers taunt her, curse her for giving up a child. The woman is respectful enough not to suggest medication. "These things . . . maybe better you pay no attention," she'll say. "I mean when they make no sense." It's the tone you'd use with a little girl who dreams she'll pitch for the Yankees someday. From the start, Louisa bought into the idea that Peggy had been some virgin boss lady, accomplished but sexless.

Louisa's good at her job, and Peggy respects that. She's unflappable when Peggy loses control. She threw a picture frame across the room last week, barely missing her brother Sean. The son-of-a-bitch had wrecked her nap with his relentless gibes. "Do you hear him, Louisa? He won't stop!" Peggy couldn't tell if she did or not, because Louisa remained expressionless. She simply removed the jar of skin cream from Peggy's grip before she could throw that too, and by the time Louisa got her back into her chair Sean was gone.

Peggy wonders if Louisa thinks she's imagining things, especially when she hums into Peggy's ear: *Everything okay, everything okay.* It's not that she's lying. Peggy knows she means well. But she tends to doddering old fools for a living, so her kindness is hardly a comfort. It only makes Peggy feel as if she's been relegated to the ranks of the demented. But the woman treats her like she still matters, and that's comfort enough.

After Sean left, Louisa spoke softly to her. "Your niece, you talk to her? You tell her the dreams?" She was patting her shoulder, something she rarely does, because Peggy's warned her not to treat her like a child. Then, in that husky whisper of hers, the one Peggy finds so endearing, she said, "Or maybe Bill?"

"And what would be the point in that?" Peggy mumbled. Bill doesn't talk about anything he can't prove, he likes the world solid, neat. Tell him how you feel and he squirms; tell him your dreams and he rolls his eyes. That's why they broke up—she's certain of that now—not the months she spent in Derry without him.

He heard she was living here in this home for the has-beens, so he comes to visit. They don't talk all that much, at least not about why her sisters and brothers won't leave her alone. It almost slipped out once, how they torment her about Nora, but he cut her off before she could finish. "You'll never learn," he said. "The more you let them bother you, the harder they'll try. It's great sport for them."

His first visit startled her. She hadn't seen him in more than forty years, not since the day he showed up at her father's wake. He'd aged so much she had trouble not staring. Yet somehow his face was the same. The lines and creases brought out what must have been there all along, the disappointment, the suspicion. And despite the stoop he seemed just as tall, his skin still tanned. She wondered if he still took those long fishing trips.

"So there you are," he said, as if he'd tried every door between hers and the elevator. The sound of his voice made her feel like a teenager, when he'd stand at her front door and greet her with the very same words, pretending she was the one who'd shown up late.

She was delighted to see him. The air from the fan lifted wisps of his white hair, and she was relieved that she'd agreed to comb hers that morning. She got to her feet, slid the humiliating walker aside, feeling not exactly graceful but at least mobile. "How did you know I was here?"

He crossed the room toward her, his gait unsteady. She wondered if he would put his arms around her, but he didn't. "Your sister, of course."

He meant Mary, the blabber, and Peggy chuckled. "Well, you certainly know how to keep channels open. She's been dead five years now."

"I do okay," he said, winking.

Peggy suspected his brother Conor must have told him where she was. Conor kept in touch with her, always had, showed her pictures of Bill's sons when they were born or graduated or got married. She was never sure why he thought she wanted to see those things. It wasn't easy for her. When Bill's wife died, Conor shared the news as if some sad chapter in his brother's life had ended and things could finally be made right.

It surprised Peggy, after the incident with Sean, when Louisa suggested she talk to Bill, because the woman never bothers with him when he's here. When Peggy introduced them, she gave him no more than a polite nod. Nora treats him the same way. Not a word. She seems to disapprove of his visits. The last time Peggy told her he'd come by, she cut her off. "He's gone, Aunt Peggy. Stop this." So she doesn't tell her anymore.

At first Peggy wondered if Nora might be holding a grudge. But that can't be. She knows nothing. Even Bill never knew she was his. Telling him would have changed nothing. The last thing Peggy wanted from him was a sense of obligation. She wanted that even less than she wanted a child.

Her sister Maureen knew that right away. She was ten years older than Peggy, but never inclined to pamper her. She came at her like a prison matron, then took the ratty kitchen towel off the handle of the stove so Peggy could wipe her eyes. "How far along are you?"

"Maybe five weeks now."

Maureen's sigh had no sympathy in it. "Well, you could take care of it the way Annie did." Annie was their cousin, lived down the block from them on Moffat Street until she left Brooklyn altogether, never came back. She had an abortion because the father was a married man.

"Please don't ask me to do that," Peggy said, looking down at the towel in her hands, twisting it until the stripes became a barber pole.

"I'm not the one asking for anything here." Maureen slammed down her cooking spoon, splashing dots of sauce on Peggy's blouse.

"It's a lot to ask. I know."

"A lot to ask?" Maureen's voice was sharp, almost shrill. "My Liam is barely two months old! How am I supposed to manage two in diapers?"

Peggy was afraid to look at her face.

"And how is Jack going to feel about bringing up this baby? Another man's child?"

Peggy moved to the table to get away from her. When she couldn't stop crying, Maureen came and sat with her. "You need to tell Bill. He'll do the right thing. He's a good man."

"I don't want the right thing." As soon as she said it, she knew she shouldn't have, and she tried to backtrack. "All I mean is I don't want to start our life together that way."

But that wasn't the real reason, and Maureen knew it. In a few weeks the semester would be over and Peggy would have her degree. She was at the top of her class. She had job prospects already.

Maureen stood, wiped her hands down the front of her apron, fingers spread wide. She stared down at her sister for what seemed like forever. "Spare me the nonsense, Peggy. It's clear as day what you don't want." That was the first time Maureen looked at her that way, with such contempt. The first of many.

Nora arrived in the winter, premature, but Maureen fussed over her and she gained fast. She sat up early, walked early. She was strong, just like her mother, with the same boundless energy. Right away they saw what a quick learner she was, devouring books just the way Peggy had. She looked like Maureen, long and lanky with dark hair, freckles—which was a blessing, because Liam never figured it out. They couldn't keep it from the rest of the family, but the secret took on the strength of an oath.

But Maureen is gone now and Peggy knows something is not right. Too much is slipping away. She needs to tell Nora. She wants to look at her and say it out loud. There's no shame anymore. Nora deserves to know who she is. I'm her mother, Peggy says aloud, and that's that, not just *someone she's always looked up to*. She hates when Nora describes her that way. This has to be made right. Nora's entitled to the truth. We both are. It's time.

•

Peggy wouldn't eat this morning, refused to be washed. Nora, perched on the edge of the bed, has her braced against a wall of pillows, but she's barely upright. Nora insists she have some tea, but she refuses. The mug is the one Nora brought her last fall after she packed up the apartment. It's Peggy's favorite. "Because I chose it," she told Nora, "not my jailors." But it's too heavy for her today, so Nora holds it to her lips.

Peggy gives in, takes a small sip. Nora wipes her lips afterward and for some reason Peggy is reminded of Fr. Redmond and the practiced way he'd wipe his mouth at the altar after tasting the wine. She asks Nora about him. "He's gone," Nora tells her, "got transferred last year to a parish three states away."

Nora lifts the mug to her lips again. "Have some more," she coaxes, but Peggy turns her face away. "Please, Aunt Peggy. Last time you did this, they had to—"

"There's something I need to say to you."

Nora sighs, sounding weary or short of time, and the mug lands rudely on the night table. Peggy wonders if Nora's afraid she'll start meddling again, try to dissuade her from traveling to Turkey on her own. "Wait," she whispers, her heart quickening, "that can't be right. You showed me photos. On your phone. Photos you took in Istanbul. I remember now." Nora was wearing a long blue scarf in one of them, the color of the azaleas in Maureen's yard. They stood here in this room together by the window. That trip is over and done with. Peggy takes a breath to center herself, but these moments, when she understands how things can slip away, leave her shaken.

Nora shifts her weight, as if she might get up from the bed, and Peggy clears her throat. She must begin, right now, because she wants her within reach when she tells her. "It happened when I was very young," she says.

Nora looks somewhat interested, and Peggy wonders if she's hoping this will be another tale of Irish Catholic oppression. Nora soaks up the family's immigration stories like a dry sponge, like a child with no roots. Maureen raised her to be *American*, as if ethnicity was like a bad smell, something you scrub out before it's detected. Peggy's mother was the same way. You're not Irish. You're American, she'd insist, hoping they'd all pass for WASPs.

Peggy's lips are parched. Licking them doesn't do much good. She needs to take it slowly, ease the shock of it. "I was young when it happened."

"When *what* happened?"

Peggy wants to be quick, but the words resist her. She has to force them. "I had a child," she says, but it doesn't come out right. It sounds formal, yet absurd, as if she's meeting with her Analytics staff, claiming she's seen the Easter Bunny.

Nora turns her head away, all but rolling her eyes.

Peggy grips her arm, harder than she intended, desperate to be heard. "A girl," she says.

"What happened to her then?" Nora says this with a shrug, as if playing along.

"I couldn't keep her."

There's no response, not even a nod, until Nora pats her hand. Peggy jerks away, so angry she can't speak, can't even swallow. Does she think I'm a child? A toddler struggling for words I haven't learned yet?

"I'm sorry. That must have been very difficult," Nora finally says, but it takes her much too long. Peggy knows she's just being polite, the way she might hold up her end of a dinner chat. She wants to strike her. *How dare she belittle me?*

"I was engaged. Engaged to Bill. I've told you this."

"Yes, of course, you did." Nora's voice is like syrup. "Of course, you did. I haven't forgotten."

"But that wouldn't have been the right way to start a life. Not with a baby."

"He didn't want the baby?" Nora seems mildly curious again.

"I never told him." The words catch in her throat, because the choice she made seems so much harsher now than it did then, inexcusable. "I went away. For months."

"Away where?"

"To Aunt Patsy's, in Derry."

Nora narrows her eyes, bites her lower lip the way she has since grade school. Peggy knows the look. It's fear. "So she's still there, your daughter? In Derry?"

Peggy takes her hand, desperate to make this happen in a way that won't bring pain. "No, Nora. I gave her away. Gave her to Maureen to raise."

Nora stiffens, jerks her hand away "What do you mean? What happened to her?" she says. Her voice is thin, childlike. "Was she sick? Did she die?"

"Wait," Peggy says, shooshing her, because she can hear them out in the hall, Sean and Maureen, arguing, and Mary too, with that cackling of hers. She can't make out what they're saying, but they're coming closer to the room. "No, no," Peggy whispers, "she's not dead." She feels flushed, frightened. She must do this now, right now, because they may barge in, try to stop her from going any further, making any claims.

Nora's eyes are watery, a rash deepening on her throat. She starts to speak but stops herself, and Peggy worries she'll lose her temper, the way she did when Maureen died, when the orderlies had to remove her from the emergency room. But Nora lets out a quick, nervous laugh and stands up. She moves stiffly, her limbs resisting her, and it occurs to Peggy—how absurd that she's forgotten—that her daughter is over sixty now.

Nora lifts the bedrail, snapping it back into place. "You need to get some rest." Her voice is flat, robotic, and Peggy can't tell what she really wants to say, but she sees that Nora has made up her mind to protect herself, pretend Peggy is no more than a precocious child, amazing the grownups with outlandish remarks.

"I should have told you," Peggy says, feeling her chances slip away. "I know that." Her tongue feels thick, the words stick to each other. "I wanted to. So many times. I didn't want to give you up," she pleads. "You've got to believe me. I didn't."

Nora reaches for her sweater, but her hand is trembling and it slips to the floor.

"I'd never have been hired, Nora, not with a baby at home. You know that as well as I do." She tries to lift herself off the pillows, but pain shoots through her wrists and she falls back.

Nora bends down for the sweater, wincing as she gets back up, muttering fierce curses under her breath, and Peggy is certain they're meant for her. "You're not making sense," Nora says, then steps away.

"Nora, don't leave."

"I'll stop at the desk on my way out. Maybe Louisa can come in."

"Nora, talk to me."

At the door, Nora glares over her shoulder. "You're not well, Aunt Peggy. Stop this. Please stop it." She grasps the door handle as if desperate to escape, as if she's come face to face with the meanest cruelty.

Peggy hears Bill say her name. He's leaning against the bureau, putting a cigarette out in the tray that holds her rosary beads. He's wearing the Aran pullover her mother gave him. It fits him well, although the stain from their last Thanksgiving together is still on the sleeve. But how long has he been standing there? Did he hear what she told Nora? "I didn't see you come in," she says, struggling again to sit up.

He raises his hand, gesturing for her not to try. "Don't bother," he says. "I won't be staying." He sounds sullen, angry, and the guilt rises in her chest like acid. She's done it all wrong again.

"I'm so sorry," she tells him. "I was wrong to keep it from you."

"She's not thinking straight today," Nora says. Peggy sees that she's talking to Louisa, standing in the doorway with her, not to Bill. She acts as if he isn't there.

"That's not true, Nora," Peggy tells her. "I *am* thinking straight. I know what I need to do. I made a mistake. I know that now." She grips the bedrails and pulls herself up. "Nora, don't go," she says, but Nora doesn't look at her. Peggy struggles for breath, the pain mean and sharp, but Nora won't help, doesn't even turn her way. Peggy reaches for her, arms open wide. She needs to hold her close, help her understand what this can mean for them. "Nora," she says, but she sees it's no use. Nora won't come to her. Instead, she moves into Louisa's arms, sobbing, her body shaking.

Peggy glances back at Bill, but he's not at the bureau, not in the chair or near the window. He's not in the room. Something's happening, something terrifying.

Peggy looks around, at the window, at the photos. Did someone put them back where they belong? She can't remember. And why is the television on? She never puts it on this early. But is it still early? The sunlight is strong. Surely too bright for morning.

She calls to Nora again but gets no response.

"Louisa," Peggy cries. "Make her listen to me." But the woman doesn't seem to hear her, even when she says it again.

She loosens her grip on the bedrail, lets herself sink into the pillows. The pain in her wrists lessens slightly, and she looks down at her hands. The veins are swollen, the skin speckled, the fingers crooked, the same way they've been for so long. There. Everything's all right. The same as it was. Nothing has changed.

But what if it has? she whispers, then glances again at her daughter, at Louisa placing Nora's sweater gently across her shoulders. What if they can't see me? What if I'm not here anymore?

THE BROKEN PLACE

A black pick-up was parked haphazardly across three spaces in the store's parking lot, the motor idling. The driver lingered at the wheel, very still, as if trying to gather himself. Dearnon, who'd been watching since the truck pulled in, put his newspaper down. The afternoon was cloudless, crisp, the kind of April day that can force a man to wonder about starting over. He hadn't had a customer all day, and he wished this one would either come in or leave already. The driver cut the engine but rested his arms over the top of the steering wheel, still not ready to get out. In the bed of the truck sat what appeared to be a huge telescope. Dearnon had never seen anything like it before.

The driver's door opened and the man stepped down. He was big, unsteady on his feet. He took small, heavy steps toward the entrance, as if uncertain whether the pavement would hold him. He wore a black shirt, black jeans, boots worn down from wandering. Thinning, strawberry blond hair was tied back in a ponytail. He opened the door of the shop without noticing Dearnon and looked toward the counter. Dearnon winced secretly at the paltry offerings: some stray beef jerkies in a display box, misshapen and gray; an empty rack meant for gum. The man's shirt was darkened with sweat, even on this mild day. He made it to the counter, leaned his weight against it. Something was wrong.

"Can I help you, buddy?"

"Hope so." He had a broad, friendly face, good looking. He placed his hands, palms down, on the counter. "In a bit of a fix." He leaned forward heavily. Whiteness mottled the freckled skin on the backs of his hands and his face was sickly pale. Dearnon worried he might be about to topple. The man tried to speak again but had trouble forming the words this time.

"What's up?" said Dearnon.

"Sweet."

"What's that?"

"Sweet. OJ?"

"Comin' right up."

Dearnon retreated to the back of the store, where he kept the drinks refrigerated. There was plenty of beer but only two bottles of orange juice left. He couldn't remember the last time he'd placed a juice order. He took them both and headed back to the counter, but he couldn't see the customer. He hadn't heard the door so he didn't think he'd left. Hurrying to the front, he felt slightly out of breath. He was gaining weight.

The big man had slid to the floor, sat leaning against the counter, knees up, head in his hands.

"You okay, fella?"

The man was barely able to raise his head. Dearnon opened the bottle of orange juice and leaned over him to offer it, but the man was too weak to hold the bottle so the storekeeper went down to the floor, braced the back of the man's head in his hand and put the bottle to his lips. He took some in, although most of it dribbled onto his shirt. Dearnon pulled out a shirttail to wipe the man's chin.

"Maybe I better call Dr. Randall. He's not far from here."

The man shook his head.

"Want to come take a seat in the back?" Dearnon slept most nights there these days, not bothering to go home. The dog was gone now too.

"In a minute," the man said. He closed his eyes and let himself relax into Dearnon's arms. This caught Dearnon off guard, and he didn't like it. Thoughts of the baby forced their way in, that same raw vulnerability. He shut his eyes, tried to remember when the Cubs' next game was, what he was going to tell the bank about the overdue payments, anything that would shut out the pink blankets and the crystal blue eyes. He'd never wanted the baby, made that plain right away. He and Irene were good together, fun. When she went ahead and had it anyway, he didn't complain, but he didn't understand, and he didn't talk much anymore. Their life became a different place, and he didn't know the language. All that mattered was the regimen of feeding and caring, except he didn't care, not the way he was supposed to, not until she got sick.

He looked down at his customer's face, but felt wrong about witnessing a thing like this, when a man's body betrays him. Dearnon settled himself down with him against the counter, tried to relax, but he was getting worried, wondered if he should get up and call a doctor. Then the big man stirred, raised his head, able to sip more of the juice as Dearnon held it for him. "I took some insulin. It'll kick in."

"Diabetes?" Dearnon said.

The man nodded and they sat quiet for a few minutes.

"You give all your customers this kind of service?"

"Not a problem." Dearnon saw they were about the same age, mid-forties.

"Is there anyone I can call for you?"

"Not a soul." Dearnon thought he heard the customer chuckle.

They listened to the trucks on the road, relentless, making their way south. Dearnon couldn't remember the last time he'd just sat with someone, not without some expectation involved, some unspoken obligation.

"I'm Ed. Ed O'Brien," said the customer, offering his hand.

"Marty Dearnon." He shook his hand. The man wore no wedding ring, and Dearnon wondered if he too was on his own.

"Is that a telescope in the truck?"

"Yup. That's Girlfriend." He took the bottle from Dearnon's hand, put it to his lips.

"You an astronomer or something?"

"Eclipse chaser. I was up in Montana. It was a beaut."

"You seen a lot of 'em?"

"My share."

"They don't exactly happen in the neighborhood. I guess you travel all over the place?"

"Yeah, you have to get on the road. I got hooked back in 1990. That summer was the first one I paid any real attention to, but I didn't see the total, wasn't in the right place. So I started to make it my business to get to whatever place had the best view."

Dearnon chuckled. "I knew a guy once who visited every major league baseball field in the country."

"I've got some unbelievable pictures. Saw one in Siberia, one in Bucharest. That was the best one."

"Why? Clear shot?"

"That, yeah. And I got to watch it with a woman I cared about." O'Brien lifted the bottle and Dearnon watched the rest of the liquid empty out.

"Feelin' better?"

O'Brien nodded. "I ought to be used to these spells by now."

"Maybe the docs need to adjust your meds." Dearnon's uncle had been diabetic, and he had asked him once if he could watch the injection. "Next time," he said. But the man was dead by then.

"Let's just say I don't always stick with the regimen."

Dearnon heard the rebellion in O'Brien's voice, the unwillingness to play by the rules. It was a dangerous way to go, but he couldn't fault him for it. He just shook his head.

"Every time things go haywire, I wonder if it's curtains," said O'Brien. "But things always settle down."

"Where you headed now? Home?"

"Not yet." He put the bottle down.

"Where is home anyway?"

"Good question," said O'Brien, with a bit of a laugh. "New Jersey, not far from Princeton."

"I been on that turnpike. After the army."

"Well, don't let that fool you. It's a pretty place really."

"Oh, I didn't mean—"

"It's okay. You own this place?" O'Brien looked at the shelves, and Dearnon wished he had a way to explain why they were mostly bare.

"The bank owns it really."

"Still, it's yours to run. That's something." His glance took the place in again. The lower shelves near where they sat held only a few boxes of Cheerios, one tipped on its side, and odd jars of relish and cans of peas. "Just open up?"

Dearnon grinned then, letting it in, the time that had passed already. "Six years." He looked around the store, wondering again if he should have bought those shelves at that auction when he had the chance. He had an urge to defend himself somehow, make it clear that things could have been different. Business had been good in the beginning. But a business like this takes time, energy. You have to want it. Before long all they wanted was a doctor who could tell them what was wrong. Dearnon said nothing, and O'Brien stopped the questions, as if he understood there would be no neat explanation for the state of things here, that the reasons were still too raw.

"So where's the next eclipse?"

"Japan."

"Is that woman going to watch it with you?" O'Brien's face changed, and Dearnon wished he could take back the question.

"She's not interested." O'Brien took a deep breath, trying to sit up straighter, but it was a struggle. He looked out into the parking lot, as if frustrated, eager to move on. "Things get pretty quiet here."

"Business comes in spurts, I guess." But it didn't. It hardly came at all anymore. Some days he didn't bother opening up. He had to sell the place, but he couldn't seem to part with it. It had become his hideout. Customers were an intrusion. A year ago, he'd dismantled the bell that announced an entry.

O'Brien didn't challenge him.

"I'm thinking about selling."

"Yeah, maybe a new location," said O'Brien. "One of those strip malls where you can get some run-off business."

From where they were sitting, Dearnon could see the dust that had balled up under the lowest shelves, and he felt oddly embarrassed, as if it could still matter. When he first opened the place, he'd polished the wood floors on his knees. He was fanatical about offering special cheeses, breads you couldn't find that easily.

O'Brien gazed at the bottle in his hand, almost as if he expected to find some kind of answer in it. "It didn't have to be this way," he said, and for a crazy moment Dearnon wondered if the man was reading his mind.

He remembered the casseroles Irene left him in the fridge, how much that had angered him, as if feeding him made her any less gone.

He left them out for the dog. "Yeah," he told O'Brien. "I know what you mean," but Dearnon never did figure out what he could have done differently, what would have been good enough, or even why he didn't at least try to talk to her. He looked out through the glass of the front door into the parking lot. He could see the telescope in the truck, the huge metallic blue barrel reflecting the sunlight. He wondered what it would be like to be able to cart around the thing you needed most in the world.

"So you gonna be there?" Dearnon said.

"Japan?"

"Yeah."

"Got nowhere else to be."

"How long since you seen her?" Later, Dearnon wondered why he didn't stop there, at a point where he would have understood nothing more about this man. Or about himself.

"Two years," said O'Brien.

Hardly enough time to forget what she smelled like. Dearnon didn't need to know any more than that, because all endings were made of the same stuff. A silence too long. A bed too big. "Ever try to reach her?"

O'Brien looked at his watch. "Twenty minutes ago."

"And?"

"She says it won't work, not now." Dearnon wondered if it was about his illness, but he waited for more, realizing he wanted a different answer, a different ending. A car pulled up outside, but then moved on, as if the driver saw she had arrived at the wrong place. Good, Dearnon thought. He didn't want to get up.

"She had this odd thing she did." Dearnon listened, not surprised that the things the man would remember would be the things he couldn't make sense of. "After we had a fight, she'd call me to see if I got home okay. Every time. I completely forgot about that, till just recently." Dearnon knew that letting shit like that back in wasn't good. "I wasted all that time." He understood then that O'Brien was probably very ill, and that he knew it.

He opened the other bottle of juice, took a slug and passed it to O'Brien, who downed the rest and sat up straighter. "What do I owe you for these?"

Dearnon laughed. "On the house." He sat up, but reluctantly. He didn't want the man to leave. The last time he'd exchanged this many words with anyone he was explaining himself to a nurse from intensive care who wanted to see ID before she'd let him near his own daughter. The child crying out to him made no difference to her.

O'Brien got to his feet, still unsteady but better than before. He gathered his things and Dearnon was struck by how purposeful he seemed, checking his watch, asking how much time it was likely to take to get to Laramie.

"Three hours, easy. You sure you don't want to rest up, eat something?" But Dearnon could see the man was gone already, his mind on the road.

O'Brien thanked him, said he'd be fine. He adjusted the straps of his heavy backpack, extended his hand. Dearnon shook it. There was no more to say. He watched him go out the door. A few steps before he reached the truck, he hesitated, and Dearnon thought he was going to turn around. But he kept going, opened the tailgate, searched for something.

He wanted to call to him, but he stopped himself. He looked down at where they'd been sitting, let his thoughts go where they shouldn't. He fought them off, concentrated instead on the stranger's truck backing up, turning smoothly to protect its cargo, then moving with only the barest hesitation back onto the road.

When there was no more to see, Dearnon locked the door, so he wouldn't be disturbed. He walked to the back, moved the newspapers off his bunk and sat down, picked up the phone. The number came to him with no effort at all. The rings were insistent, shrill. He wished he could stifle the sounds, keep them from making so much out of this. The hello was small, tentative, as if she'd recognized the number. He didn't speak, and she hung up.

He said the number aloud, as if testing it, and this time the sequence began playing tricks on him. Maybe that wasn't the number. Maybe that wasn't her.

EVERYTHING NICE

The hair on Mad Dog's headpiece sticks straight up and the teeth show like he's in permanent attack mode. My job is to let out a howl every time the Bulldogs take the ball down the court or make a basket, and the crowd howls along with me every time. The Mad Dog costume is too big for me, made for a guy. The heavy jersey gathers in folds at my neck and down the back of my legs, so I look more like a bloodhound than a bulldog, but it doesn't make any difference to the kids in the stands. The more I trip over my own paws, the more they like it.

The team's official mascot is a year ahead of me, a junior, but I've known him since grammar school. He was desperate to study for a history test, so I agreed to fill in—once he swore to tell no one.

The coach calls a time-out, and I feel my phone vibrate again. That's the second time in fifteen minutes. I scurry under the bleachers to the exit on the far side of the gym and run out into the hall, then duck into the locker room. I lift the headgear off and dig the phone out of my bra. Two missed calls, both from Irene, my little sister. No messages.

Pressure starts building behind my eyes and now my head hurts. What if Irene is alone in the house with Dad. I'm sticky with sweat. I try to shake off the fear. My brother Sean is grounded, which means Irene's not alone with him. She's fine. But she's been staying by herself too much, hardly says a word. In the mornings sometimes her eyes are red. She won't talk to me, not about Dad. So I'm scared. Irene is ten now; he started with me when I was nine.

I don't want to think about all that. Not now. I want to hear the kids cheering for me again. The headgear is heavy but when I put it back on it calms me down and I head back to the game. I like being invisible. I'm good at it. In a classroom or at the dinner table, I can fade away in plain sight.

Mr. Cassidy, one of the Phys Ed teachers, is patrolling the perimeter of the court, so I keep Mad Dog's antics politically correct. But he'll step outside soon enough. He's a big guy with a big appetite and he can never stay away from the refreshment stand for a whole quarter. Sure enough, he slips out for a snack, so I scamper up to the opposing team's star center—sitting at the end of the bench—and make a show of beating on his head, scratching him with my plastic claws. The fans love it, on both sides of the gym. Even the star is laughing.

"Here comes Cassidy," someone yells. I slip under the bleachers, heart thumping as loud as the ball on the court. I'm giddy, high really, maybe from all the attention or maybe just from the risk of getting caught.

"Get out here," Cassidy yells. "Get out here right now." I can barely hear him over the noise of the crowd. He bends over, reaches into the space between the lowest benches, his huge forearm a tight fit, his face blood red, mustard dried into the corners of his mouth.

The kids in the stands take Mad Dog's side, shouting, "Good doggie! Good doggie!"

My giggling ricochets inside the headgear. I hardly recognize the sound. It feels strange to be silly, to be part of something that's just for fun. My phone vibrates again, and the fun's over. I have to get home.

Sean's car isn't in the driveway, and I'm trembling so bad it takes me three tries to get the key into the front door. My saliva tastes like acid. I coax the heavy door open so it won't creak, stand motionless in the landing, trying not to breathe. I listen for something out of place—a footstep, a cough, anything that might help me figure out where my father is.

Sean was home when I left for the game, grounded again. He threw a punch at Dad last night, drawing some insane line in the sand. Not a smart thing to do here, not if you want to keep all your teeth.

Something heavy hits the floor upstairs. A book? A shoe? I can't tell. The cat doesn't like it either. He slinks out from the shadows of the family room at the bottom of the stairs, prances past me on the landing. I follow him up to the main floor, then tiptoe along the narrow hallway, as skilled as he is at not being heard.

The door to Irene's room opens and my father leans halfway out, as if checking to see if the coast is clear. He's in his denim work shirt, his face ruddy, and he's squinting, even though the light in the hall is barely bright enough to make out the wallpaper pattern. The skin on the back of my neck goes cold, and I realize I'm grinding my teeth. I hate him. I want to corner him, make him explain what he was doing in there.

He steps out, sees me, and we both freeze, locked like hunter and prey, each waiting for the other to make a move. With a grunt, he glances away. Then, head down, pressing himself close to the wall, he trudges down the hall toward the kitchen.

"You're in. Good," he mumbles as he passes. That's our good night. I gag from the smell of drink and cigarette smoke and something else I can never name.

It's dark in Irene's room, and the air smells bad, heavy with something it can't fully absorb. I don't want to breathe it in. Irene's in bed, covered in thin strips of flickering light coming through the blinds from a street lamp that's been dying for months. She lies still, her winter quilt of white unicorns and pink maidens pulled up to her neck, a pillow over her head. I say her name, but she doesn't answer. I flip the light switch on, move closer to her, but she burrows deeper into the bedclothes, presses herself against the wall.

I sit down on the edge of the bed, put my hand on her back. She squirms, moves as far away as the wall will allow. "Irene," I say. No answer. "Re." Nothing. I slide the pillow away, pull the quilt down. She's trembling, her nightgown inside out. Her dark hair, wet at the temples, is sprayed wild across the pink sheet, as if she's been tossing and turning for hours when it's barely past her bedtime.

I touch her arm. Stiff. Muscles tight. "What did Dad want?" She doesn't turn to look at me. "You called my phone."

She mumbles something into her pillow.

I put my hand on her shoulder, try not to sound upset. "I had missed calls from your number."

She lifts her head slightly so I can hear her. "I wanted to see when you'd be home," she says, her face chalky white, tearless.

"Well, I'm home. So what's going on?"

"Nothing," she says, burrowing back into the covers. "I'm tired."

I want to believe her, but I don't. Maybe Irene thinks I won't understand, that I don't know what it feels like to want a world to end.

The sounds from the kitchen are inescapable, the fridge closing, the swish of a beer can pulled open. I ask her again if anything's wrong. Still nothing. We've been through this before, twice in the past three months. I can't get her to talk. Maybe it's better that way, because I have too many questions, all of them ugly, and I don't want to ask them.

I get up, cross the room, flip off the Cinderella light switch on her wall, the one that used to be mine. "Leave it on," she says. "I want to read." I put it back on, watch her reach for her book. It's thick, with a shiny plastic library cover. I spot a bruise on the inside of her forearm and my stomach tightens.

"What happened to your arm?"

"Nothing."

I move closer to get a better look. "What happened?"

She pulls her arm back under the covers. "Please. I'm fine. Just let me read."

"You don't look fine. How did your arm get like that?"

"I want to read." She opens her book, finds her page.

"Will you talk to me tomorrow? We can go to Dairy Queen."

"I can't. I have a math test."

"Irene, tomorrow's Saturday."

"I forgot," she whispers, peering over the top of her book, as if to see if I believe her.

I want to. I want to be wrong, but no kid forgets it's Saturday. "Okay," I tell her, "so we'll go?"

"We can't. Tomorrow's Timmy's Communion party."

Timmy is our cousin, a sweet kid, at least he used to be. I haven't seen him in a while. The family doesn't get together that much anymore.

"Right," I mumble. "Well, Sunday then."

She nods, and I let that be enough.

In my room, I undress by the moonlight coming through the window. I avoid mirrors. At least fifteen pounds of me have nowhere to go. I wear my clothes loose, a pathetic camouflage. I like Sean's shirts and sweaters because they reach my knees. In bed I pull the blanket up tight under my chin, try to think about exams, about whether I'll finish my history paper in time. But thoughts of Irene won't go away. I'm scared.

Scary is a constant in this house. The air is charged with a low-grade panic, like you've left a hot iron facedown or a candle burning. It's like that, but bigger, scarier. Anything can set Dad off. A fork hitting the floor is enough to make us all run for cover. I'm sixteen now, and it's been this way for a very long time, like I've stepped off a curb to find a car coming at me. But it's more than a flash of terror; it's a way of life.

I'm better now at staying out of his way. He hasn't come into my room in three years, hardly even looks at me. When I was little, we did stuff together. We went places. I was his favorite. Sugar and spice, he called me. He even played dolls with me. I'd pretend I couldn't get the baby to sleep and he'd rock the doll in his arms, sing songs about Irish freedom in a voice that made me think being oppressed was romantic. Later, when there were no more songs, when I woke with my eyes crusted from tears, my stuffed animals crushed into the foot of the bed, nobody asked any questions. Nobody looked out for me.

Irene became his sweetie. She sat in the front seat with him almost everywhere we went. At Christmas, only the Santa at Macy's in New York was good enough for Irene. Sean and I had to settle for the skinny guys at the mall. Irene has always been special to him in a completely different way, so I have a hard time believing he'd hurt her. He really loves her.

The wind picks up, branches scratch the window. I hear Sean get in around eleven and raid the fridge, then go to his room. It's almost midnight when Mom gets home. She's a nurse, works the evening shift. Her steps are soft on the stairs, then closer. My door opens and she leans in to check on me. She always looks in on me first. Sometimes I wake to the touch of her hand on my forehead. It scares me, until I realize it's her. She'll smile at me, as if I'm someone important she recognizes from long ago. Maybe she thought I was special once, before I got older. Maybe she loved me. But I can't feel it anymore.

I keep still, pretend I'm sleeping. I know I should talk to her about Irene, but I can't do it. He'd know it was me who told on him, and he'd make sure I paid the price. And my mother would find a way to blame me for whatever happened next. And what would that be anyway? How could she stop him? Who the hell do you tell when your husband's a pervert? The police? And if he goes to jail, what happens to the rest of us? How do we pay the bills? What do we tell the family? What would I say to my friends?

My door closes and I kick the blankets away. The air in the room is so dry it makes me itch. My skin feels like plastic, as if it's not my own. I pull a pillow over my head, try to remember the words to the poem we talked about in class today, the one by Mary Oliver, about her bones feeling the taste of water, like it's something they've never felt before.

One by one the bedroom doors open and close as Mom makes her rounds. Finally, she heads toward the kitchen, and I hear water running. She's probably making her tea. I can't lie still. I feel like a coward, like his accomplice. I get up, put on my robe. Maybe I'll just see what kind of mood she's in. I'm not sure where my father is, so I open my bedroom door just enough to peek outside. No sign of him, so I tiptoe down the hall to the kitchen.

My mother is at the counter, and my appearance in the doorway startles her. "Seosaimhin," she says. I like when she says my name in Irish—SHOW-siv-een. It's usually a sign of a decent mood. But she sounds down. "It's late," she says. "You'll be tired in the morning."

"Can't sleep."

"Try counting your blessings. You'll sleep."

She always says that. I used to actually try it, until it got too hard to think of any that I wouldn't trade for a chance to escape. The kettle begins to hiss and she turns the jet off before it can whistle and disturb the others. I sit down at the table and wait for her to finish. She asks if I stopped at the dry cleaners and whether I remembered to make the dentist appointment for Irene. But she asks in a half-hearted way, as if she has something else on her mind.

She comes to the table with her mug, the cream-colored one with *Mom* circled in shamrocks, and slumps into the chair across from me. She seems tired. "Tough shift?" I say. She looks away, so I figure she doesn't want to talk. I can't help feeling sorry for her sometimes. She works eight-hour shifts, and my dad doesn't pick up much slack at home. I feel guilty, maybe I could do more to help, but the whole business wouldn't be half as hard if she could settle for a single thing being less than perfect. Until a year ago, she was still ironing our T-shirts.

"Mr. Bianco . . . " Mom finally says, barely audible. She doesn't finish, but I realize what must have happened.

"Died?"

She nods.

"I'm sorry, Mom." I know she likes the old guy. He's been in the hospital so long he's like a staffer. I even met him once. He didn't seem very likable—raspy voice, lumpy grumpy face. But she talked about how he made the new patients laugh, telling them he'd have been released long ago if the hospital hadn't lost his paperwork and his good kidney.

"Were you with him?"

She shakes her head, slides her mug away, rests her forearm on the table. "He was gone before I got there."

I see that's not the way she wanted it.

"His son was coming out next week."

"The one you've been calling? The one in Chicago?"

She nods.

"Did Mr. Bianco know he was coming?"

"I was going to tell him tonight." Her voice catches in her throat, and I have to swallow hard. If I start crying, she'll get annoyed at me.

Mom troubles over things like this. Bringing people together, before it's too late. She says when people are dying, their bodies aren't what hurts the most; it's more like they're haunted by something they've done, or worse, something they should have done.

I can't think of any way to make her feel better, so I tell her again I'm sorry.

She gets up, as if she didn't hear me, opens the dishwasher, finds the dishes still dirty. "You mean to tell me no one thought to turn this on?"

No one means me. "I forgot."

"That doesn't help." She makes it sound like her only ally has deserted her. She rearranges some of the dishes, puts the soap into the little bins, and gets the machine started. Then she takes the burner racks off the stove for washing. I've already done them, but that doesn't register. I wonder if there's anything I can do that will ever be right, be enough. I want to say something about Irene. Maybe not all of it, but something.

"Mom?"

"What?" The word comes out sharply, like a slap, like this interruption better be worth her time. That's when I see that whatever I tell my mother, however I describe what he might be doing, will be inadequate, beyond anything she'd recognize as possible.

"I was just thinking about something."

"About what? What is it?" She stops wiping, smacks down the sponge.

Where do I start? With the bruise? With her nightgown inside out? Or with *my* first time, when we got home from Grandma's, tired from the long drive, and he put me to bed? With the places he touched me that night? "Nothing," I mumble.

"It must be something. Tell me." She stands near me at the table.

I can smell the hospital on her, medicinal and harsh. I can't look at her. "I don't know." I take a napkin from the holder and fold it, then fold it again, and again.

"Jo, what is it?"

"I don't know what's wrong," I tell her, the same thing I told her years ago, when she first noticed the stains on my sheets, the stains he'd made. I wanted to talk to her back then, ask her why he did those things, but I couldn't imagine how it would make any more sense to her than it did to me.

Mom sighs, goes back to scrubbing the racks, every last spot, every little greasy smudge I missed. Every rub feels like an accusation.

"I did those already," I say. *Pay attention to me,* I want to scream, *not your stupid chores.* I get up, move closer to her. "Mom, Irene's got a bruise. On her arm. Did you see it?"

"Yes, I saw it." She answers without looking at me. "And so did your father. He's furious."

"I don't understand."

"He called me at work. Sean was goofing around—you know how she likes him to spin her around till she's dizzy? I've warned them a thousand times it would end in tears."

My shoulders sink, the tension in my back slips away. Maybe Dad didn't do anything. Maybe he was just checking on her. "But Sean wasn't here when I got home."

"He was here long enough to mess things up again. That's why your father's so angry. He cut him some slack, let him go out, then he got a look at Irene's arm. He's at the end of his rope."

That could be what happened. Sure, it could. I could be all wrong. Mom is practically wringing her hands, but I can hardly keep from smiling.

"Wait till he hears about the trouble at school. Your brother better wise up. One more screw-up and your father will throw him out. I know it."

He's made that threat more than once, but when Sean hit back last night, bloodied his lip, I knew Dad meant it.

"I can't cover up for him this time. He hurt someone. It's bad."

"Yeah, I know," I say, but it isn't that bad, not really. At least it's no worse than what he did to that kid after math class last month. But maybe the school has had enough, maybe because so many people witnessed it this time, even an assistant principal. It happened right outside the gym. "But that fight wasn't really Sean's fault," I tell her. "I saw what happened. That kid was asking for it."

"That's always Sean's story."

"No, Ma. It was Andy Belkin. He's the one who tormented Terry's little brother all last year. He's a bully." He's also the guy who put his hand up my sweater after the game with Toms River. I was coming out of the girls' room when he strutted up to me. I thought he was doing his usual where've-you-been-all-my-life routine, the one he does when he can't find some other trouble to get into. But he was close, too close. In a few steps he had me pressed against the lockers, groping me. He didn't see Sean. Neither had I. One minute Andy was grunting at me, the next he was on the floor, blood all over his face. All he had was a bloody nose, but if I hadn't pulled Sean off of him, it would have been a lot worse, because Sean was in a rage.

"Bully or not," Mom says, "I've got to tell your father about it tomorrow."

"It's not fair."

"Never mind that. You go to bed," she says. "I need to finish up here." Her hands look raw, as if she's already used them too much for one lifetime. They're not pretty hands, but I like how strong they are. She's never hit me, not ever; she has other ways to shut me down. I picture my friend Terry's mom, her perfect nail polish, her flawless skin, the part-time job she blows off when she pleases. The first time my mom had a manicure was last fall, for a cousin's wedding. She pledged it would be the last. I think the joyful color embarrassed her.

I kiss her good night—a light peck on her hair that I'm sure she doesn't notice—and go back to my room. I pick up my phone out of habit, put it down again. I can't focus. I should ask Sean, knock on his bedroom door and find out for sure what happened with Irene. But I stop myself. I'm making something out of nothing. Dad would never hurt her that way. It's different with Irene. He cares about her.

I move to the window, open it. The air smells like rain is coming. I can hear Sean's TV, a Giants game. He and I don't hang out together anymore, not since he left middle school, but we still talk. He's almost two years older, taught me how to ride a two-wheeler, lets me use his surfboard, shows me where Mom hides the extra candy at Easter. He's kind to me when Dad slaps us around, but now he's hitting back, and it's scary because Sean is a big guy. I tell him he's crazy to do that, but he says he's not putting up with Dad's shit anymore. Empty words, really. Dad has all the cards.

•

Dad can't find the tie he wants to wear. It doesn't take much more than that. A missing shoe, an empty scotch tape holder, that's all the reason he needs to go on a rampage. Ordinarily, I grab Irene and get out of the house, but we only have ten minutes left to get ready for Timmy's First Communion.

I pull Irene into my room and close the door. "So what do you think of my new backpack?" I say, trying to distract her from the arguing in the hall.

"I like it," she says. "Same as I liked it two weeks ago." She gives me a sad smile, because she must know why I'm asking.

Dad barrels into Sean's room next door, and we both get quiet. Dad's made up his mind that Sean took his tie. Sean hasn't worn a tie since *his* First Communion, but logic isn't part of the picture when Dad gets this way. The shouting gets louder, meaner. Finally, Sean screams back, the moment Dad welcomes, because then he can use his self-righteous anger as a cover for what he wanted to do all along. It's a family ritual. He lashes out, leaves Sean humiliated, bleeding sometimes. Mom cleans his cuts afterward, warns Sean not to start with him. But her voice always trembles and I can tell she's afraid of Dad.

Something heavy hits the wall, probably Sean, and there's one last curse from Dad. When it's quiet again, Mom opens my bedroom door, holding a shirt out toward me. "I need you to iron this for Sean," she says. I take it and go to the hall closet for the iron. Sean is in the bathroom, dabbing his nose with a wet towel. There's blood on his shirt and a heaviness in his shoulders as he leans over the sink. In the mirror, I see the familiar look of defeat on his face. He notices me there and kicks the door shut.

I hate the way Dad leaves us feeling, like we've lost before we've had a chance to fight, like we've lost ourselves—because when he's finished with us, we don't get to lick our wounds. No pouting. We take our punishment and get back into the swing of things, like the whole business is no more than a bad cramp.

I iron Sean's shirt, he gets dressed, and we pile into the SUV and drive eleven miles without a word. Sean sits on the other side of Irene in the back seat with me, staring out the window. He's breathing through his mouth, still dabbing at his nose.

Uncle Neal spots our car and walks up to greet us as we get out. Dad hikes up his pants—the way men do when they're about to talk about something they own—and strides toward his brother, saying "I'm telling you, it's taking them longer and longer to make themselves beautiful these days. But you be the judge; tell me it's not worth it. Are these girls prettier than ever?" Dad puts his arm around Mom and Irene. I stay out of reach.

Uncle Neal gives him an *amen*. "You're a lucky man," he says. He's wearing a suit that doesn't fit him anymore, and the tie around his neck is loose, like it's there for form's sake. I climb the church steps with Irene, Sean close behind, all three of us wanting distance from the grown-ups. Even church is preferable to listening to them repeat their tired lies about how glad they are to see each other. One pew in the back of the church is half-empty, so we slip in, weaving clumsily around the knees of the people who won't slide over. Mom and Dad come into the aisle, scope for seats up closer but give up, settling for spots across the aisle just ahead of us. Mom does her deep-knee-bend genuflection and a slow-motion sign of the cross before getting into the pew.

I hate seeing her do that. It's laughable when gray-haired old ladies of the Rosary Society do it or the stray nun you see around sometimes, but when my mother does it, my stomach knots into a fist. Maybe it's because the Church has nothing to do with our lives—or hers—except for the inconvenience it causes on Sundays. Mom respects all the wrong things. All week she treats her daughters like galley slaves, but faced with her bully of a husband or a church pew, she becomes suddenly reverent.

I brace myself, because this isn't going to be easy, having to watch my parents *oooh* and *aaah* at rows of angel-faced kids receiving the body of Christ. The procession starts. The kids' steps are awkward and uneven, and they look like they wish they could scratch their noses or get out of their stiff new shoes, or at least make everyone stop staring at them. But no one can resist. They're perfect: the shine on their faces, the innocence, that wide-open look in their eyes. They have no clue what they're innocent of. I watch the girls, try to catch a glimpse of each little face, see if I can find one like me, one who knows already what guilty feels like. I glance at my parents again, knowing they'll be cooing at every child that goes by. Mom is in tears from it, but Dad isn't looking at the children. He's searching my face, looking all forlorn. Maybe he can't find what he's looking for there, maybe he can tell that whatever connection he thought he had with me is lost for good.

But I doubt he ever thinks about me, about what he used to do. I hate thinking about it. There are long stretches when I don't. That took a long time. When I finally realized he wasn't going to do it anymore, I tried to pick up where I left off. But I couldn't. I'd forgotten what it felt like to be normal, not to wait for him, not to slip off my panties when I heard him in the hall, so he wouldn't tear them. Some days seem almost normal now: school, friends, chores, homework, a great chocolate cake, a good movie. Normal doesn't last that long. I'll remember a feeling, a smell. The details are disconnected, and mostly I can't put them together. But the fact of it returns, and I'm branded, back to being someone at fault, someone in hiding, afraid people will figure it out.

•

We got home from the Communion party much later than we planned. Every party in the family ends with a we-really-should-get-together phase, and this one took longer than usual for my parents to worm out of. Dad's drinking made him downright chatty. I stood a distance away, by the car, saying nothing, trying to figure out what to do, whether to tell someone what I saw at the party.

I kept an eye on Dad all afternoon, even following him around from a distance. The party was in the hall of a rescue squad building. Dad's family can't fit into anybody's house anymore. Too many cousins and now their husbands and wives and little kids. But even all those people weren't enough to keep Irene safe.

On the second floor, above the hall, there's a room with big couches and chairs, where the squad hangs out when they want to relax. I didn't know what was up there until I saw Irene coming down the stairs, looking red-faced and sweaty. I asked her what was wrong, but she strode past me, mumbling something about a toothache. I started after her but Uncle Liam, moving in like a drunken linebacker, whisked her away to dance before I could get to her.

Then I turned and saw Dad walking from the direction of the staircase. I didn't know for sure whether he'd been up there with Irene, but I had a bad feeling, so I went up to see what was there. When I saw the huge couch, I lost my balance, had to lean against the wall. Irene's party balloon, the one Aunt Margaret had given each of the kids, the one Irene wouldn't part with even while she was eating, was suspended against the low ceiling, the string hanging limp, the shiny white oval tilted against the beam, as if on a noose.

•

I wake to the sound of my Dad's voice. It's loud, coming from the kitchen. For a second I can't get my bearings. I'm lying across the foot of the bed, no covers, no pillow, still in the clothes I wore to the Communion. The room is dark. Then I remember rushing in here when we got back, throwing myself on the bed. I must have cried myself to sleep.

Irene had nothing to say in the car on the way home from the party. She sat there picking at her nails, until Sean asked how she bruised her arm, whispering so only she and I could hear. She shrugged, as if it was something that couldn't make a difference, couldn't be changed. Sean seemed confused, but I wasn't, not anymore.

I turn on my side, listen hard, but I can't tell where Dad is now. I get up, crack open the door, hear him talking. He's still in the kitchen.

"Enough already, Anne," he says. His voice is harsh and gravelly, a tone you'd take with a dog too stubborn to train. He mumbles something I can't make out, then gets loud again. "If you don't do something about him, I will."

"Lower your voice," Mom says. "Please. You'll wake the whole house."

"Fine with me. Let him come out here and explain how we're going to pay that kid's hospital bills."

"The boy is fine. He didn't even need stitches."

"I've heard enough."

"For heaven's sake, be reasonable."

"I'm warning you. Shut the fuck up about it."

I flinch, imagine him squaring off to hit her.

"Why can't you—" Mom's words are cut off by a bang and a clatter, maybe a chair hitting the floor, and a high-pitched yelp from Mom. He curses again, then tromps down the stairs to the family room.

Why does she put up with him? It's insane. Why do any of us put up with him? I picture myself shouting in his face, telling him it's over. That I'm going to the police, to Uncle Neal, to the neighbors, somebody, anybody. There's got to be a way to stop him. My hair has come out of the clip and I reach up to fix it, but I'm shaking and I fall hard against the dresser. My hip hurts and my eyes are burning. I straighten up and go out into the hall. Mom is in the kitchen, standing at the counter, holding an icepack to her temple.

She's hurt. Her back is shuddering and I know she must be crying. I take in a sharp breath, angry at her for putting up with him, but she doesn't hear me, doesn't see me pass.

At the top of the stairs, I grip the banister, afraid I might fall, because I can smell him, or maybe I only imagine it, that stink he leaves in his wake when he's drunk. The TV is loud, a car dealer shouting about low prices. I want to confront him, demand an answer, but my knees lock. I'm scared. I picture Irene again—the tangled hair, the bruise—force myself to go down. I stop as I reach the landing, where I can see down into the family room. He's in his recliner, his body bent forward, both hands around a can of beer, cooling his forehead on it.

I close my eyes, because I can't move. The carpet under my feet is like wet sand, sucking me down. It's always this way when the memories come. Exhausting. I can never actually see his face. Only the feelings come back, my cheeks wet from his open mouth, the drooling, the disgusting drooling, the struggle to keep from breathing him in, and the weight, heavy and immovable, the sense of being pressed into the mattress, pressed into the floor, into the earth, the darkness.

His voice breaks in from downstairs. "Who's that?"

I don't answer. The recliner groans, leather squeaking. He must be getting to his feet.

"Who the fuck is up there?"

I sink down onto the bottom step, holding my breath, afraid my mother will hear him.

"Answer me. Anne? You want to start in again?"

I don't move. I hear him land hard into the recliner. My head hurts from the pressure behind my eyes. I can't do it. I can't face him. I climb back upstairs, ashamed of myself, go into the kitchen to try again with my mother, get her to listen. She's not there. And what can I say that she'd be willing to believe?

I drag myself along the hall to the bedrooms. Outside Sean's room, I sink onto the carpet, my head in my hands. I hear Sean's TV, commentators trading barbs and pointless predictions, the unending bombardment of football stats, sliced and diced for yet another record breaker. They defend their teams as if a moral cause was at stake.

I let my head fall back against the wall, close my eyes, and the TV's dissenting voices circle me, become something else. I remember the howling Celtic warriors Dad used to tell us about, steeling themselves for battle, pounding their chests, shaking their long wild hair, holding their weapons high, ready to die. And I see a way to stop him.

Sean will help me. I know he will. He'll stand up to him. I picture Sean raising his fists, knocking Dad down. My heart races from the thrill of it, and I reach for the doorknob, pull myself up, knock softly.

"Yeah?" Sean says, and I open the door. He's lying on his bed, knees up, his phone resting on his chest. His shirt is open, one foot is bare.

When he sees it's me, he looks relieved. Maybe he thought it was Mom knocking. Then something shakes him—something about my face, maybe, or the way I'm holding my hand against my stomach—and he sits straight up, then gets to his feet, already poised to spring. "What happened? What's the matter?"

I step inside, close the door behind me. Even as I say the words—*Something's happening to Irene, something you need to know*—I picture what will come of this and I know it's not the answer, not the right way out. It will destroy us as a family. I should go back to my room, back to the secrets. It would be safer that way, at least for Sean, but the urge to stop my father, to hurt him, won't let go of me. I can't turn back.

"What?" Sean says. "What is it?"

I can't say it.

"Irene's arm," he says. "Dad did that, didn't he?"

I nod. The movement is slight, almost imperceptible, but he sees it, and my panic eases—like a terrible storm weakening—and I glimpse, even in the wreckage, the peace of ending it.

THE LAST OF THE DARLIN' BOYS

Even from the foot of the stairs, Maureen smells it. The drink. The unmistakable odor of trouble that emanates from a brain pickled in spirits. The better choice would be for her to go about her business, put the groceries away, dust a bit, let him sleep it off. She's seventy-three now and the stairs sometimes make her hips burn. But she takes off her jacket, goes up anyway. She wants an explanation.

She finds her grandson Brian tucked under the navy-blue comforter in the bedroom she lets him use. Hardly bigger than a walk-in closet, it remains his, whenever he needs it, no matter how many unplanned turns his life takes.

But it isn't always about need. Even now, in his late thirties, Brian sometimes just wants to be with her, the way he did when he was little, when he'd plead with her to come and get him. Danny, Brian's father, her firstborn, roared and stomped when he was in a rage, like a wrecking ball spinning from the center of the place, leaving his wife, Kate, sprawled on the carpet somewhere, one more casualty in the chaos of smashed lamps, broken dishes, and trembling tots clutching crib railings or hiding under beds.

"Grandma, come get me," Brian would whisper into the phone, his plea as familiar as a rosary, and she would.

The bond between them came like something unexpected, a wish she didn't know she had, a vague hope that she might get it right this time. The years passed and at Maureen's lace-curtained house Brian could play Metallica and Nine Inch Nails at the highest tinny volume her stereo could manage, and when she got home from work and the neighbors complained, she'd turn her back to them, mutter about how tolerance was a lost art.

The tiny room is stuffy and still, no movement beneath the comforter, even after Maureen speaks his name. A bottle lies empty beside the bed, along with the glass from the upstairs bathroom. The blinds are open, morning sunlight everywhere, but the window is closed, which surprises her, because Brian makes a mission of letting air into the house when he visits, sometimes even when it's raining, as if desperate for some kind of equilibrium between where he's been and how it feels inside.

Bitterness rises like acid in her throat, and she struggles with what she'll say to him. He'd been sober since the accident, almost four weeks, the longest stretch in years. She steps closer to the bed, not wanting to see his face but convinced she has no right not to. She believes she's somehow responsible for what's become of him, not just the wild Irish DNA he inherited, but her inability to find ways to steer him in another direction, her readiness to cover up his mistakes, even when they were deadly. She's watched him fight the drink and lose, watched his innocence recede, until, to others, no trace remains of anything but guilt, a guilt she'd hoped to spare him.

She wonders if the accident haunts him, as it does her—that moment when she pulled him away from the young girl's side, a girl who was surely dead, just a slim, small figure tangled in a shrub, barely noticeable in the thick pinks of spring. The swerving tire tracks darkened the road, marks of desperation. Her bike landed yards away, the breeze ruffling the happy pastel streamers on the twisted handlebars. Nothing to be done. The area was deserted, a bucolic country road; no houses marked the horizon. She'd appeared without warning. It wasn't Brian's fault. If they'd reported it, he would have been blamed. Because of the drink on him so early in the day.

Brian lies flat on his back, eyes closed, arms outstretched and palms up, like a crooner finishing a ballad. She places her hand on his forehead, but he doesn't move. He may have passed out, but would he look like this, so pale and slack? Drinking can do that. She saw it with her husband, with her father, with Danny. But Brian is resilient, the type who gets himself to work the morning after. His embrace can make you believe a boss will change his mind, a car isn't really totaled.

She says his name, but he doesn't respond, so she says it again louder, then grabs his shoulders to shake him. Nothing. Frightened, she takes his hand to feel for a pulse, but she's shaking so badly she can't feel anything. She crouches next to him, turns her head to rest her ear on his chest, trying to hear his heart beat. She's not sure she does, but she thinks she feels his chest rise, and she prays he's breathing. She gets up, stumbling, and heads downstairs to get her phone.

By the time the ambulance arrives, she's upstairs with him again, and she must go back down to get the door, her legs weak and uncooperative. She follows the emergency team up the stairs, as if they know how to save him, though she's surely the most experienced in this parade of rescuers.

•

Maureen glares at the nurse, impatient for her to go away. She's slow, cursed with poor posture and a pursed mouth from too many shifts spent in drunk tanks. Maureen has seen her type here before, possibly the very same woman. She finishes her routine at the next bedside, unsurprised by anything she's found, and pulls the thin, beige drapery back into place. The cold, indifferent sound of the metal rings along the pole mocks the need for privacy.

Brian's eyes are closed. He looks restful, and Maureen is relieved he had no seizures this time. Her great-grandson Eric stands beside her at the bed railing, so tall for fifteen, staring down at his father. "Dad," he says.

Brian grunts, opens his eyes. Maureen's hair is pulled up, and harsh light from the ceiling filters through the loose, gray tendrils. "Goddammit," he chokes out, a lame attempt to shout. "What's he doing here?" He pounds his fist into the mattress, points a shaky finger at the door, insists Maureen take him away.

"He's your son."

"I said get him out of here."

Eric has seen his father in this condition before, but as Maureen walks the boy out, she hears his breaths coming in little shallow gasps, as if he's discovered something he's powerless to change. She knows that feeling, the shock of it. It returns often now, unexpectedly, as raw and desperate as it was the moment she saw that the girl's blond hair was matted with blood, that her leg was obviously broken, that she couldn't possibly survive.

Outside the room a long metal bench rests against the wall and Maureen tells Eric to wait for her there. She watches him lumber over to it, collapse against its rigid back.

She returns to Brian, her pale lips pressed together to keep from saying what she learned long ago is pointless to tell a drunk. How can you treat your son this way? She holds on to the bed railing. She wants to sit down, but Brian doesn't ask her to. All he wants to know is the time.

"The time? *Now* you're worried about being late? You should have checked your watch twenty-four hours ago."

"You had no business bringing him here."

"Eric *is* my business. And he ought to be yours."

Brian clenches his fists. "You shouldn't have brought him here."

"Keep your voice down, for Chrissake. He'll hear you. He's right outside."

"Why would you do something like that?"

"He was worried. He wanted to see you." There is some truth in that, but there's more to it. Eric is suspended again. Fighting. This time with tenth-graders, older but not bigger. One of the boys needed two stitches from falling against a drinking fountain. Eric is six-feet already, eyed by the football coach, who encourages him to stop cutting classes, get passing grades.

"So you bring him to a place like this? The smell alone is enough to—"

"He hasn't seen you for two days. He was scared." Nothing in her tone sounds apologetic. Maybe that's why she gets no answer. "So was I," she adds, though she suspects it will make little difference to him right now.

She's scared for Eric too. She knows he counts on her to defend him, forgive him, just the way his father did, and Danny before that. Brian grew brazen in the luxury of it. By junior year, he was bringing his friends to her house, boys his mom didn't approve of. A few of them were older, served in Afghanistan right after high school, and when they returned, they introduced him to a different kind of trouble—hard drinking that led to short stints in nowhere jobs. But he parted ways with them before things got too bad, went to college, started traveling. The Midwest. Canada. Short stays in small towns where odd jobs lay around like leftovers.

Brian would come back to Brooklyn, describe what skies were like without buildings in the way, roads as quiet as the woods beside them, the smell of wild vegetation, the sight of places undisturbed by the rules needed to govern greed and desire. He liked the Northwest, the mountains. He brought a woman home, lovely and lost, carrying his child. Maureen did not welcome this change and disguising it was pointless. Brian could tell, because she kept her distance from the girl, a tall blonde Nordic type, too quiet, too pliant. Maureen wanted Brian to be happy, but this girl was a spark that would never catch. She wondered how long it would be before the girl could take her eyes off Brian and see how far off course she'd gone.

Maureen sought time with the baby alone, as she had with Brian. The girl stayed until the child was two, just as lost as she was at the start. Maureen quit her job until the boy could start preschool. She treasured those months, though they took a toll on her back. Eric—she hated the name—was big for his age and always pleading to be picked up, such a darlin' boy. Maureen obliged him, wanted him to feel protected.

Brian pushes the sheet aside, as if to get up. "What time is it, for Chrissake?"

She steps back to get a better look at the clock on the wall above them. "A little after three," she tells him. He's already back on the pillow, wincing from pain.

"Shit." He digs his palms into his eyes. She sees there's more bothering him than a bad pint.

"What's going on?" she says. The fellow in the next bed, no more than four feet away, stirs again. His moaning has been nearly constant. "Are they short on morphine here, or what?" she mumbles, glancing in the neighbor's direction. Brian's muffled laughter comes out like a snort.

Maureen plants herself in the chair beside the bed. "So," she says.

"So?"

"So he thought you'd show up at his game yesterday, with Kate."

"I didn't make any promises."

"That excuses it?"

"You hear me making excuses?"

"No, because there aren't any."

She feels her face get hot. The motherly concern she felt for him when they brought him here this morning has morphed into something else, something that makes her want to shake him. How could she have expected him to realize what he'd done, how he'd hurt his boy needlessly? She wants him to be sorry for that. But that's not the way he treats his mistakes. He's become like his father now. The rare apology, if it's offered at all, is given in passing, buried quickly in excuses. Even after the girl was killed, his regret seemed like an afterthought. "*You* should have driven home, not me," he wailed. "If you weren't so afraid of the fucking interstate, it never would have happened."

The moaner in the next bed calls out someone's name. "Joanie . . . Joanie . . ."

"Does he never stop whingin'?" Maureen mutters.

"Joanie . . . Joanie . . ."

"She's gone out for cigarettes," she tells him, twisting to look over her shoulder. There's a woman at his bedside now and beside her a young girl with hair so blond it startles her, because it's tied back in something blue. Just like the girl they left on the road.

"Dad," the girl says. "It's okay. It's me, Joanie. I'm here."

Brian looks over at her, and Maureen wonders if he sees it too, how much she looks like the girl on the bike. The pale hair, the white hoodie. The dead girl's was unzipped and twisted around her shoulders, darkly blood stained.

"I'm here, Dad," Joanie tells the man again, but her voice trembles as she reaches for him. They've strapped the man down to keep him still and she seems uncertain where to touch him. She takes her father's hand in hers, then lets it go, as if so small a tenderness is not enough. She leans forward, places her hands at his temples and kisses his forehead. Maureen can't bring herself to look away—even when the girl begins to sob, even when the woman tries to pull her off the man. The girl jerks away from the woman's grasp. "Leave us alone," she tells her. Sobbing, she wipes her eyes, smearing mascara across her cheeks, like a toddler who's gotten into her mother's make-up bag.

"Look what you've done. You need a tissue." The woman digs into her bag, cursing under her breath, unable to find what she wants.

Maureen spots a box of tissues on Brian's night table and gets to her feet. She takes the box to the far side of the man's bed, where the two are standing, offers them the tissues.

The woman takes the box and looks away, mumbling a thank you, but the girl meets Maureen's gaze. Her eyes are very blue, glistening from tears. "You're very kind," she whispers, still crying, and Maureen feels something twist in her chest. She wants to answer, but she can't move, can't take her eyes off the girl, such a fine, delicate thing. What right does God have to inflict such pain on an innocent child? What right did Brian have? She nods to the girl, because she still can't speak. The girl smiles, as if she recognizes who Maureen must be, a harmless old lady, who only means well. Maureen turns away from her, fearing she'll lose control, confess the truth. I'm not very kind, not kind at all.

Maureen lowers herself carefully into the chair at Brian's bedside. The pain in her chest softens, spreads warm and mean through her stomach. He stares at her, examines her really, and she wonders if he'll finally say something about the accident after all this time. "There's something I better tell you." He speaks tentatively, as if testing the strength of an old plank that might not bear his weight. She's afraid he's about to blame her for what they did, claim he, at least, was too drunk to think straight.

"What is it?"

"It's about Dad."

"Danny?" She doesn't want to hear it.

"He had an awful lot to drink."

"Is this supposed to be news?"

"Gran, you need to listen. This isn't good."

Maureen folds her hands in her lap. No, with Danny, it can't be good.

"We were drinking last night. Together. Into the morning."

"And what did you think would come of that brilliant choice?"

"Gran."

She clasps her hands more tightly together, willing herself not to scold him. But she wants to. She wants to tell him to look at this girl, this Joanie, and see what he's done, see the Joanie they left twisted in that shrub.

"We wound up at Bully's, his old haunt in Bay Ridge, near the freight yards." Brian takes on a far-away look, as if picturing the scene. "He was okay at first, spewing his shit about Trump, comical really. People were laughing at him."

She knows the place. Danny has taken him there before. He took him there the night of the accident, insisted he'd never seen Brian so upset. Danny knew nothing about what happened that day. Neither did Kate. Maureen had sworn Brian to secrecy. By the time the girl was found—late that night—Brian had already had the car detailed. Maureen insisted that might not be enough and later paid for the Honda to be repainted. A story ran in the paper, naming the parents, their son, the girl—Brittany. She was fourteen, finishing eighth grade. They lived in Mamaroneck. Maureen found a phone number online of the place where the mother worked. She entered the number in her Contacts list but never called it. The clipping is still in her wallet, tucked neatly behind her license.

"What possessed you to go with him—"

"Will you listen? When I got to the house to pick Mom up for the game, he was giving her a hard time, really cranking it up."

"About what?"

"Does it matter? I figured I'd take him out, let him cool off. We had some time. We'd make it to the game by the third inning." Brian scrapes his hands over his face, rubs his palms into his eyes, as if that might help him explain. "But in the bar he started in about Eric, about Mom. I was pretty drunk by then myself. He got loud. They made us leave. So we walked over to the yard, sat in a freight car."

"How did you get into the yard?"

"He knew the guard. He's been there for years, since before Dad left the job. We sat talking with the guy for a while. Dad told him he wanted to walk me around inside, show me where the barges come in to load the containers. It was like he missed the place. So we sat there in a freight car."

"So what's all the fuss about?"

"He fell asleep."

"In the freight car?"

"Yes."

"And you left him?"

"I must have."

"Well, he'll wake up soon enough, find his way home. He's staggered home from there a thousand times."

"And what if he doesn't? He's got no—"

"So what?" She wants to curse him, demand to know how leaving a brute like Danny in a stupor could be worse than leaving a child for dead on the side of the road.

"He'll wind up on the barge, for fuck's sake. That car gets loaded onto the barge in an hour. He'll wind up in Jersey City."

Maureen's laughter is so mocking and so loud the rest of the ward goes silent until the nurse's footsteps clop toward them. Maureen stands up. There was a time, not so long ago, when she would have helped her son, gone to the yard to get him, save him once again from his own mess. But she can't do it. She has to stop this.

The nurse appears at the foot of the bed. "We need to keep it down," she says, and Maureen wants to laugh again, ask her if a good joke isn't exactly what this place needs.

"For fuck's sake," Brian mumbles.

Maureen gives the nurse a glance imperial enough to send her away.

"Your father will do well in Jersey City," she tells Brian.

"He hasn't got his inhaler with him."

This piece of information, this detail of Danny's carelessness, makes her chest tighten with fear as she pictures him desperate, struggling for breath. But anger rises and her jaw tenses up. How are some allowed to live a life of unlimited neglect? Somehow they figure out that others will take care of business, keep them from having to face the pain they cause, face any consequences at all.

"I'm sure half of Brooklyn is worried sick about him," she says.

"Gran, think about Mom, what happens to her if—"

"I've got more important things to take care of. So do you."

"I'm fine, for Chrissake."

"Happy to hear it. Your son's not."

Brian raises himself onto his elbows, his thick brows nearly meeting, and Maureen is reminded of her brute of a husband and the look he'd take on when he suspected something hadn't gone his way. "What do you mean?"

"He's suspended. Fighting again." She crosses her arms, instinctively ready to defend the boy, though she knows Eric could have avoided it. He's told her the truth, that he knew the boys were afraid of him. He could have walked away. "I'm heading up to school after this to meet with the principal."

"O'Connor?"

"Himself."

"He's an asshole."

"No question. He's also in charge of deciding if we have to send Eric to public school. This is his second suspension."

"O'Connor is a lot of hot air. It'll all blow over. They're hungry for every tuition dollar they can get."

"And what if it doesn't? Would it hurt you to show some interest?"

"I need you to get over to the yard, get Dad off that train. If you leave now, you can get there in time."

She recognizes that tone—the same one Danny would use, and her husband—there's no mistaking it, the certainty that she'll do as she's bidden. "What a relief," Maureen says, pulling her sweater closed. "If I head out now, I can save the day."

"What the hell's gotten into you?" Brian hisses.

She glances over at the girl. She's sitting on the edge of the bed, shoulders slumped, quiet now. Maureen turns to Brian one last time, because she knows what she needs to do. She looks for a sign, any indication, that he might be ready to do something for his son, for the girl they killed. "What shall I tell Eric?" she says, positioning the strap of her bag over her shoulder.

He rubs his head. His hands seem stiff, his fingernails dirty. "About what?"

The question stuns her. How did he become so callous, so self-absorbed? Was this her doing, bit by bit, the excuses she'd offer, the asylum she'd provide? "About the girl, the one we left in the bushes," she says. "What shall I tell him about that?"

Brian narrows his eyes, as if her image has blurred. She's tempted to let the silence speak for her, but that won't do. "We have to make amends," she whispers.

He lifts his head from the pillow, braces himself on his elbows again. "What the hell are you talking about?"

"I'm talking about that child. Her parents."

"For fuck's sake, it's over and done with."

"It's not over for me. Or for them."

"Stop it," he tells her. "Just stop it."

"I'll go then," she says. And before he can say any more about Danny, about anything, she's at the door. Gone.

The air in the hall is cooler, fresher. But there's no one on the bench. She calls Eric's name, then calls again, before moving down the hall to the exit. She digs in her bag for her phone, finds his number. "Where are you? Call me."

She's outside on the sidewalk when he returns the call. "Where are you?"

"Home," he says, and she thinks he might mean her house rather than his own. It takes her a second to realize she does not want that. She knows she should remind him they're expected to meet with Principal O'Connor in less than fifteen minutes. Instead she waits, wondering if he'll say it first.

"Should I come with you to the yard? I heard Dad ask you to go to the yard for Grandpa."

She pictures Eric outside the hospital room door, listening to his father worry about a man who gets a hard-on from hurting people, like his father before him. She feels heat rising in her chest, in her neck. Her throat tightens. How well they think they know her. How predictable she's become.

She watches the people passing the hospital, a man in a flannel shirt, holding a box on his shoulder; a woman pushing an empty stroller, a child skipping alongside her; a young man walking two large, unruly dogs. The wind is picking up, the sky a white gray.

"I'm not going to the yard," she says.

"Why not?"

"Because it's none of my business."

She's sure Eric is stunned by this, puzzled. Normally, she would feel compelled to explain. But she's already past that. Her complicity is undeniable, a stench she can't bear to breathe in anymore.

"Mr. O'Connor is expecting to see you. If you leave now, you can get there in time. Tell him your dad had to go to the emergency room."

"By myself?" She hears the sharp breath he takes in. "Aren't you coming?"

"No."

"It wasn't my fault, Gran. They're always blaming me for stuff."

Fault. How irrelevant that idea has become to the men in her life, how integral to hers, stalking her, owning her. "You can tell Mr. O'Connor that."

Eric hangs up on her. She pulls at the neckline of her sweater to relieve the tightness spreading across her chest. She struggles against calling him back, but she doesn't.

She joins the passersby on the street, the random parade of people moving along, set on their errands, their appointments, their chores for the day. She feels unsteady, uncertain, but she steps into the entryway of a small bookstore, an enclave from the wind that's getting stronger. She wants to be sure she'll be heard. She clicks on her Contacts list, scrolls down, finds the mother's number, and makes the call.

THIS LIFE

The biting wind lifted the woman's hair across her face, so Alan could see only her chin and a bit of her nose before the bus came between them, hardly time for the shock of it to register, barely enough to be certain. He stood with the little crowd that had emerged from Penn Station, waiting in the stubborn slush to cross 7th Avenue. The woman was on the other side of the street, leaning out from a doorway, one of those gray entryways tucked between two stores, a door not meant to be noticed, drab filler between garishly decorated storefronts. She wore a long coat he thought he recognized—beige with a silky red lining—and she seemed to be staring at something in the distance, as if expecting someone who should have arrived by now. Her hair reached her shoulders, wild and directionless. Dark, lengthy roots surrendered abruptly to a frosted blond, marking a boundary, a time when she must have cared how she looked. The bus took forever to pass, and when it was gone, so was the woman. And so was the young man's certainty that it was his mother.

The woman looked homeless, ragged, and Alan couldn't imagine his mother that way. She'd been gone five months, since just before his fall semester started at NYU. She left no note. Her passport was gone and the boots she wore to walk the dog, but all her luggage remained in the closet, her jewelry undisturbed. His father went through the motions of trying to find her, but not for long. Her absence became Alan's ugly, unrelenting companion, a torment and an accusation. Guilty and confused, he'd study the ceiling in his dorm, unable to sleep. He'd drink, smoke weed when he had the money, imagine her alone and sick somewhere, dead even, but never like this, like someone despised. Even at his sister's funeral, back in May, she'd looked good. A friend from school remarked on it, but it was nothing Alan hadn't expected, because that's the way she always looked. She'd arrive at the hospital outfitted perfectly, even at the end, when Eva couldn't open her eyes anymore. His mother had stopped speaking to him by then. When he entered a room, she left it. He'd driven her daughter into a tree, and at the funeral, she ordered him out of the limo. The silence in the car swelled from the shock of it, until Alan obediently opened the door. "Patricia, that's so hurtful," his father said, a lame intervention.

She let herself sink into the leather, turned her face to the window. "What difference does it make?" she said, as if that argument had long since been settled. Alan didn't want to believe that was how she felt, even when she seemed so indifferent about his injury from the accident. She went to the hospital only once after the surgery on his hip. When he told her he didn't think it was healing right, she told his father to look into it, but his efforts were minimal. Alan gained weight, stopped playing tennis. The pain never fully subsided and the weed he smoked did little to ease it.

When the light changed, Alan failed to move with the crowd. His head was still at home in New Jersey, the house smelling of Douglas fir, the front porch twinkling in darkness, the mantel missing two stockings, the dog given away. Eva's room was another guestroom now, the furniture replaced, her posters removed, her friends' photos gone. He remembered sitting on the edge of her bed, a few nights before the accident, as she listened to him sort out feelings he had no name for, his feelings for Rosa, a girl who'd never been on an Honor Roll or a college campus, a girl who worked with an apron on.

Throughout the Christmas break, he spoke very little to his father, and never got around to telling him how many courses he was failing, or the reasons why. He'd wake too tired for class after roaming the streets in search of his mother, or too hung over to focus. He saw no point in college anyway, not for him. If he wanted a job, his father would find him something. Don Meyer was a self-made man, president of RenVo Holdings, a financial firm with tentacles everywhere.

And now there was Rosa, Alan's secret waitress girlfriend. His secret girlfriend who remained in the shadows even though his disapproving mother was out of the picture. At first she was just a lovely comfort, someone easy to be with, eager to please rather than judge. Eventually, he told her what he'd done, that the accident was his fault. The confession did not repel her, and gradually she challenged him, offered him a different way to feel about what he'd done. "Are you crying for Eva? Or for yourself?" The question hurt because he didn't understand yet what she was asking him to see, that he would have to change or he'd lose Eva—and his mother—again and again.

Still, he kept Rosa in the background, a secret who was more than likely carrying his secret child. He didn't know for sure yet because he was so shaken he hadn't answered her calls since she'd gone to a doctor to confirm the drugstore test.

"Oh, shit," he'd said, as they watched the two pink lines appear. "That's all I need."

"Maybe it is," she whispered, turning away. He watched her tuck the tester into the book on her night table, pictured her returning to it after he was gone, treasuring it.

He went home for the holiday break without a word to her, then blocked her calls. He knew she'd want the baby and he was afraid he'd lose her if she saw how panicked he was. Decisions this weighty had never been left to him. He'd perfected the art of acquiescing, disguising resentment. Being a father seemed alien, something he had no right to. He planned to see Rosa this morning, first thing, before his first class, try to explain. He prayed the test had been wrong.

"You havin' a tough day?" someone said. It was the old fellow who manned the table to collect donations for the homeless, smiling his toothy smile.

Alan laughed, seeing that the light had turned red again and he'd have to wait. "Bad spot for daydreaming," he said. He'd forgotten the old man's name, but he noticed he'd reclaimed the spot where the Salvation Army's Christmas Santa had been. He wore the same suit he wore every time Alan saw him, a thin faded wool that must once have been a dark gray, now with a thick sweater underneath. The man just nodded, and Alan felt the same awkwardness he always felt at that point in their exchange, when he'd deposit his dollar into the huge jug and return a greeting.

He wished their charitable ritual could have remained the way it started, when he saw him infrequently and didn't feel obliged to pull an earbud away to hear what the man was saying, when it never went beyond a nod. But by April last year Alan was coming home every weekend to visit his sister, already on hospice care.

The light turned green again, and Alan limped forward, his hip pain flaring, then halted, realizing he should ask the man if he'd seen the woman across the street. "Excuse me, did you notice a woman standing in that doorway over there—about that tall?" He held his palm face down at the level of his shoulder.

"You having some trouble there?" the man said, motioning toward Alan's hip.

"It's nothing," Alan said, the same thing he'd told the paramedics after they'd gotten Eva into the ambulance. "I'm fine." But he wasn't. The pain was often as intense as the images of his sister. So silent. So broken. Sometimes Alan welcomed the pain, when it got bad enough to empty his mind of anything else.

The man's name came to Alan then. "Hermie," he said, "maybe you noticed her? Hair was all messed up. You know, roots and stuff."

Hermie pushed his glasses against the bridge of his wide nose, but had no answer.

Alan shrugged, feeling the need to explain. "She was standing in that doorway across the street. Had on a long beige coat with a red lining." He swallowed hard, afraid he might lose control. "Pretty disheveled looking."

"You talkin' 'bout Patsy? She got a coat like that."

"Patsy?" His mother's name was Patricia. No one ever called her Patsy.

"I see her around now and then. Sure. Not today though. Sorry, son."

Hermie had never called him that before. *Son.* He must have felt sorry for him, and Alan's face went warm. Maybe something in his voice had given him away. Describing his mother's appearance as anything short of perfect did not come easily.

"Never mind," Alan said. "Thanks anyway."

Hermie's look was unsettling, as if he had questions he didn't want to ask. "You can cross now," he said, motioning toward the traffic light.

Alan nodded and tried to keep up with the crowd, but a few steps from the curb, a thick-necked man in a tight-fitting coat, a bulldog of a man, stepped into his path. His bulging attaché case caught the strap of Alan's gym bag, and he had to skip after him in the slush to keep from losing it. But the big man stormed ahead, pulling the bag and Alan to the ground. Most of the crowd swarmed past as he stared up at them, cursing under his breath. As the traffic reclaimed the avenue, he struggled to get to his feet and a blaring SUV shooed him toward the sidewalk. Stragglers from the crowd stood around him and he realized he was down again, his body twisted, hip throbbing like a bad tooth, warning of worse to come. A girl standing on the sidewalk had his gym bag. She looked like Eva. Exactly like Eva. She wore a long green sweater, like the one Eva had worn on St. Patrick's Day, on the night of the accident. He watched the girl pull her hair back nervously, the way his sister had as she got into the car with him that night, asking again if he was okay to drive. "Just one beer," he told her, but that wasn't true. He thought of the blood on the dashboard, on her face, the moaning as she spoke his name, how she seemed to resist him as he tried to pull her out of the car. But this girl's face was unspoiled, no stitches, no swelling.

Alan closed his eyes, braced himself against the pain spreading through his back, and made up his mind to get up. By the time he got to his feet, the girl was gone, the gym bag left on the sidewalk. He walked toward the bag, picked it up, surprised his back didn't hurt from the weight of it, and headed down 32nd Street toward Herald Square, where he'd get the subway downtown. He thought about Rosa, hoping he'd see her at the restaurant near the subway stop at school.

Half a block ahead something caught his eye, a flash of red disappearing into a building. He quickened his pace, glancing into doorways he'd never noticed before. He stopped at one of them, the door shiny black, recessed, with no sign on it. He wasn't sure if this was the one she'd entered, but he stepped onto the little square landing, tried the metal handle. It was locked. The street was fairly crowded with pedestrians, their footsteps silenced by a pneumatic drill starting up a few yards away, but no one seemed to notice him. A few yards farther along, another door appeared, this one dark blue, paint chipping from wood that framed a dirty square of glass. He stepped closer and looked through it. A hall beyond was dimly lit, but he could see a staircase leading up to the next floor. He tried the metal handle, heard a click, but he had to press his shoulder to the door to get it open.

The air inside smelled like cat pee and grease, like the garage where his grandfather used to get his car fixed. Alan stood still, his heart pounding. A colorless narrow hall beside the staircase led into darkness, but from upstairs he could hear the faint sound of someone humming.

A dim light sprayed the landing at the top of the stairs and he headed toward it then froze as his steps wakened the old wood to a menacing creak.

"Is that you?" someone called. A man's voice. Alan remained still, waited for him to speak again. Nothing. He continued his climb, holding the banister this time. The surface felt uneven, decades of paint had bubbled and thickened. His throat felt tight and he struggled to take a deeper breath. The air tasted heavy with grit and he couldn't keep from coughing.

"Who is that?" the man called.

Alan said nothing, climbed a few more steps. Before he reached the landing, something scurried along the base of the wall, into the shadows at the end of the hall. Not far from the top of the stairs a door bearing a makeshift sign that read *Satellite Angels* was slightly ajar, and Alan moved toward it. "Hello?" he said, his voice barely more than a whisper.

"It's too late now," a man said. "You were supposed to get here an hour ago." The door opened a bit wider and Alan heard heavy, sloppy footsteps, as if someone wearing his work boots untied were moving away from the door and back into the room.

Alan put his hand to the door, pushing it open to let himself in. A tall, wiry man with gray unkempt hair stood in the center of the room, his back to Alan. He wore saggy jeans and a loose white dress shirt that didn't seem right for him, as if a stranger might have picked it out, mistaking him for someone with somewhere to go. The place was poorly lit. Boxes and shopping bags, most hand-labeled *canned food* or *toiletries* or *paper towels* lined every wall and crowded the floor space, leaving only a narrow path for navigation into the next room, connected by a wide doorway. That room had two windows, with blinds drawn. Bright sunlight forced its way through broken slats and reflected off a speckled mirror above a dresser. The bedposts cast peculiar shadows on the wall as if moving on water.

"Excuse me," Alan said.

The man turned toward him, his cloudy eyes taking the young man in as if he expected nothing new. "The truck was here on time. More than I can say for you. The driver was circling the block."

"Sorry. I'm not—"

"There was nowhere to park. He couldn't wait any longer," the man said. He was a homely fellow, made uglier by his bent nose and the grotesquely impatient expression he wore.

"I don't know what you mean. I'm not—"

"We have to reschedule the pickup." The man turned his back to him and moved to a small table, bare except for what appeared to be a list of items, several pages thick, and a lamp with a dusty, yellowed shade. The lamp was lit but the bulb so dim it was pointless. The man picked up the list. He held the papers close to his face, as if in a comical imitation of a nearsighted old man. Alan was reminded of Rosa's father, repeatedly misplacing his reading glasses, how his wife and daughters would tease him. Their bond seemed a tangible thing. It would stay with Alan long after the visits, the care they took in being with each other, the gentle way they passed a serving dish or paged through their photo albums. They seemed to know the world to be a fragile, precious place.

"You're new," the man said, turning toward Alan again. "I can see that. But if you're going to help load this stuff, you need to get here on time." His voice wasn't harsh, just uncompromising.

Alan tried to explain. "The door was open downstairs. I heard you call."

The man studied Alan's face.

"I'm looking for someone."

He nodded, as if he understood something now.

"I saw her on 7th Avenue. Just now I thought I saw her enter the door downstairs."

"You must mean Patsy?"

The name made Alan's throat tighten. "I . . . I don't know," he said.

"Have a seat." The man gestured toward the table, with its two wooden chairs. "We can talk." He spoke the way Alan's high school basketball coach would have spoken before a tough game, a warning of disappointment ahead. He was the first to reach out to Alan after the accident, offering to talk, saying, gently, he knew a good therapist. "Suit yourself," Alan's mother told him. "Words are easy. You've got exams coming up. Try focusing on that for a change." She was probably right, but drinking kept him from having to choose.

"Come on. Sit," the man said, pulling a chair out for Alan. "You look a little pale."

Alan didn't want to sit down. He didn't like this place. It had so little light. His mother used to tell him how he loved the sunlight as a child, even as a baby. He would get upset if she closed the blinds on hot sunny days. But he wanted answers, so he moved to the wooden table and sat down. The chair legs were thin and unsteady, the back hard.

The man sat down across from him. "My name is Pete," he said, extending his hand across the table in greeting.

Alan shook it. "I'm Alan. Alan Meyer."

"You're a student?"

"Yes, I was headed for the subway downtown. That's when I saw her."

"NYU? Is that your school?"

"Yes," he said, though he never thought of NYU as his. It was his mother's choice, her alma mater. He hated the place as much as he'd hated his high school and its top-of-the-heap reputation. He had posed as well as he could as the student everyone expected him to be, hard-working, sights obediently set on a promising future. Eva did the same, but it came easier to her. She was smarter, able to charm her way through situations she didn't like. And maybe for her it wasn't a pose. Maybe she saw something waiting for her at the end of the obstacle course. Alan saw nothing, wanted nothing, except maybe to be left alone, to have five minutes when he didn't have to prove himself.

"Who is it you're looking for?"

"A woman. Early fifties, about five-four, hair to her shoulders, kind of frosted, at least it used to be." Alan felt something at his back as if he'd leaned on a wet towel, but saw nothing on the chair when he turned to look.

"Sounds a lot like Patsy. What do you know about this woman?"

Alan didn't like this. His mother had always been a very private person. She never talked much about herself. When Eva went into a coma, she didn't even tell her in-laws until the third day. His father argued with her about keeping things secret. "We don't need any more thoughts and prayers," she insisted, but Alan wondered if something else was going on, if his mother was somehow ashamed of what was happening. Her Eva, her pride and joy, was now scarred and disfigured, her strength lost, her beauty gone, and now even her consciousness compromised.

"I wish it was me, not her," Alan told his mother.

She was silent, as if there was no need to respond, no need to say it. Then she did. "You're lying."

"I don't know anyone named Patsy," Alan told Pete. The air in the room felt heavy, his breathing shallow and difficult.

"Well, how do you know this woman, the one you saw on the street?"

"I think she might be my mother. She's been gone since August."

"What do you mean *gone?*"

"She just left. No one's heard from her."

"And you think you saw her?"

"Yeah, but I'm just not sure, because my mother would never look . . . like that." The care she took in the way she dressed—the color of her nail polish, the way she tied up her hair—baffled Alan as a boy. Not just the transformation she achieved—which other mothers didn't seem to bother about—but the idea that she would trouble so much with how she looked, even when she was dropping him off at school or a game. Later he hated it. The mascara, the shiny lipsticks, the blush on her cheeks were the paints she used to craft a fiction about her worth. In truth, she'd bounced from one foster home to another as a child. To this day, Alan didn't know who her real parents were, though he was convinced that she did.

She fussed just as much with Eva, who seemed to love the attention. But nothing about her son was ever right enough. His hair, his clothes, his attitude, nothing passed muster unless she'd chosen it.

"Then what makes you think it's her?" Pete said.

"I don't know. There was something about her face. And the coat she was wearing. My mother has a coat like that, with a bright red lining." Alan wondered if she might have given the coat away in one of her grand gestures.

"Listen," Pete said, then paused, as if unsure how much he should say. "Tell me how much you know. I mean about what happened to your mother." His voice had a certain force in it that Alan found hard to counter.

"I don't know anything," he insisted. "I don't know where she is. No one does."

The last time Alan saw his mother—the August afternoon her staff took her out for a farewell lunch—she wore a tailored suit in a burgundy so deep it made him think of the robes of royalty. She'd resigned from Phoenix, a huge New York fundraiser dedicated to fighting poverty, claiming she needed to work with the homeless on the street, not from behind a desk. Her access to New York's got-bucks gentry had made her the organization's top money draw for more than a decade. Brian, her closest friend at Phoenix, told Alan later that he'd left the luncheon with her, that she was quiet, too quiet, but he assumed she had a lot to process. Her daughter was dead barely three months, and he knew she'd finally split with her husband, a man whose deference for wealth was outweighed only by his contempt for the indigent, a state he considered optional.

Alan still called Brian every week, hoping she might contact him. The answer was always no. So he'd wander the streets of the city—the places transients favored, the doorways before dawn, the parks after sunset—desperate to find her, beg her to come back, start over. He'd talk to vagrants, bag ladies, hoping they'd encountered her.

"Was she sick?" Pete said.

"No, she claims she's never even had the flu. She acts like she'll never die." When the doctors proposed taking Eva off life support, his mother refused. "You're sentencing her to die." She spoke the word as if the act of dying was disgraceful, inexcusable, as if there were another choice the doctors refused to see, as if her daughter's injuries could have some other outcome.

"No, I mean was she depressed, anything like that?"

"I guess she must have been. I mean first my sister died. Then she and my dad finally split. But she'd never let anyone see that. Never."

"Did you?"

"I . . . you know . . . yeah, I could tell. She was missing work, not returning people's calls. My dad said Phoenix was ready to replace her. Then she gave her notice." Alan knew she'd stopped taking her meds. Rummaging for cash, he'd found the bottle tucked in a coat pocket, still nearly full, weeks after they'd been prescribed. He never asked her about it, never told his father.

Pete placed both hands on the table, the tips of his fingers touching, clearly hesitant to say more.

"So have you seen anyone with a coat like that? Was she here?"

"If you mean Patsy, she was here today, but very briefly. She's been coming here for quite a few months. Off and on. But she's not well."

"What do you mean?"

"She's unstable. Mentally. The first time she came, she said she worked for the city, had ideas for helping with the distribution. She carries this notebook. Always writing furiously. Taking notes. She said she had the go-ahead to revamp the whole system, but she had to study it first. But after a while, I could see. I mean none of it made sense. And she started to look kind of, I don't know, bedraggled."

"So she said she was put in charge of this?"

"She made it sound that way, but I called the city. I couldn't find anyone who'd ever heard of the program she talked about. I've asked around, Googled the name she gave me, but I couldn't find anything.

"But she keeps coming by?"

"Sometimes she'll stay for a long while, mostly we wind up chatting about politics, family stuff now and then. Other times she rushes in and out, like today, like she's late for something important."

"What family stuff?"
"She's vague, says she had children, but they both passed."

The skin on Alan's neck went cold. Had she truly given up on him, sentenced him? "What else did she say? About the children?"

"Not much more than that really."

"What name did she give you?"

"Walczewski. I'm not sure of the spelling."

"That's her name." Alan stood up, his legs now as weak as the chair's. "That's my mother's maiden name."

"Wait. Sit."

"I've got to find her," he said, but the words seemed like a line in a play, like something a good son would say.

"Look at you. You can barely stand up."

Alan moved away from the table.

"Look at you," Pete said, this time pointing a finger at Alan.

Confused, Alan looked down at what he was wearing, feeling again a dampness at his back. Twisting his jacket around, he saw that parts of it on one side were discolored, darkened. From the slush in the street? He pulled it open slightly and saw patches of blood along his side. He felt no pain but now he wondered if he'd been hurt worse than he realized. He felt light-headed, frightened.

"Where does Patsy live?"

The old man gave a hopeless shrug. "I just don't know."

Alan stepped closer. "She must have mentioned something. Some place where she stays?"

"I'm sorry. I don't know where she goes."

Alan cursed himself for the relief flooding him. He feared for his mother, his guilt even heavier now, like a shroud, but he didn't know if he could look at her again. He wondered now what good would come of finding a woman who didn't want to be found, who considered him dead. He wanted to get away from this man, be outside. Maybe he could reach his father, do that much at least, tell him that she was wandering the city.

He grabbed his gym bag and left, stumbled down the stairs. Outside he reached into his pocket for his phone, but it wasn't there. A search through every pocket and the bag turned up nothing. Maybe it's on the street, where I fell, he thought. He headed back to 7th Avenue, searching the sidewalk along the way, in case he'd dropped it somehow. When he got to the avenue, the light turned green and he crossed slowly, trying to spot the phone. Nothing.

As he neared the curb, he heard someone cry out, "Oh, my god. My god." Hermie stood, tipping over his folding chair. He held his hands to his face, pulling down the thick skin of his cheeks, as if to contain himself. "Look at you, boy," he said, staring wide-eyed at him. "I thought for sure you was dead!"

He looked as if he'd been crying or was about to, and Alan wanted to reassure him. "Dead?! You've got the wrong guy. I'm right here. I'm fine." But even as he said the word, he knew he wasn't, and hadn't been for a very long time. The end had come slowly for Eva, painfully for all of them. His own end had begun almost as far back as he could remember, unfelt by anyone. As a boy he'd had glimpses of a life he could enjoy, a self he wouldn't despise. The deadening came gradually, with no visible injury, until the only feeling left was shame.

A smile—broad and unstoppable—overtook Hermie's face. "Well, I'm sure 'nuf glad to know you're not dead," he said, almost hopping in place.

Hermie extended his hand, and Alan took it, the broad palm, warm and callous. The strength of it spread up Alan's arm, pulling him toward something, a choice. He thought of Rosa, her luxurious dark hair tied back, her dark eyes, the kindness he hadn't earned, the tolerance he didn't deserve. He could almost feel her smooth skin under his hand, her belly with its tan lines and her lovely hip bones. And now maybe a tiny life had begun. He wanted to see her, to apologize for not calling. She'd understand how hard it had been for him to be at home for Christmas, the house crammed with reminders of so many barren years. Rosa always understood. He needed to find his phone, to call her, to tell her she was right. He wanted life, a new life.

"I can't find my phone," Alan told Hermie. "Have you seen it? I think I dropped it when I fell." He glanced down at the table, thinking someone might have given it to Hermie to hold on to. The big jar was rather empty and Alan couldn't remember if he'd put in a donation earlier. He had only two twenties in his wallet and he couldn't afford to part with one. He dug his hand into his coat pocket and felt for coins. His three quarters landed soundlessly on the dollars in the jar, and he looked away, embarrassed at his paltry contribution. "That's all I have," he said, but Hermie nodded too slowly, as if he knew that wasn't true.

"I'm sorry," Alan mumbled, ashamed of the lie. He pulled out his wallet, removed the twenties, rolled them up and slipped them into the jar. "I'm sorry," he said again, more distinctly this time. It felt right to say the words out loud, without hesitation, the way he should have said them to his mother after the accident. Instead, he waited, mute and stubborn, spoke them softly, privately, only to Eva, whom he was never sure could hear them.

"Bless you," Hermie said, holding up his broad hand, and the gesture reminded Alan of a benediction, a kind of forgiveness. "You've got the light now. Go ahead and cross over."

"Yeah, I've got to find that phone," Alan said. "I'll see you next time."

"Next time," Hermie agreed, and gave him a small salute.

Next time. The words stayed with Alan as he crossed the avenue again, scanning the pavement for any sign of the phone. But as he glanced down the street where he'd seen his mother, he had a sense that there would be no next time, that he would not see Hermie again, or his mother, because he was never coming back here. He would talk to Rosa, make something right. He could be with her, with his baby. He was going to change things, leave school, maybe even the city. He wanted to do something else, anything else. He'd leave this life behind, the one his mother had chosen for him, and find another way to be.

THE BEGINNER

Keira watched the deliberate way her mother moved each paper from one pointless pile to another—figuring out which bills could be put off—and saw that nothing would change her mind about continuing the dance lessons. Keira finished drying the dishes, put the towels back on the rack, evenly folded, exactly the way her mother insisted they be hung. A poorly hung towel could trigger days of lamentation. When she had them just right, she promised herself she'd never hang a towel in that room again.

Before the sun rose the next morning, before anyone in the apartment was awake, Keira set out for the bus station in Journal Square, with her ballet slippers, her tap shoes, and the few other possessions she cared about stuffed into her brother's huge duffel bag slung over her shoulder. By the time she got on line for the bus, she was sweating, though the day was still cool. She dropped her bag in the spot behind a tall guy with a guitar case and a knapsack. He had blond hair and freckles and looked old enough to be out of high school. He wore jeans and a fatigue jacket. The other people on line were mostly men wearing raincoats and carrying briefcases. Keira's father used to get the bus here. But he was out of the picture again, had been for months, since the day before she turned sixteen. She wondered how long he'd be away this time, how long before he returned to take things out on her mother and the emergency room became their home away from home again.

The bus pulled up hissing and wheezing, and the line straightened itself as the passengers got ready to board. Keira's stomach felt loose and her hands were sweaty as she gave the driver her fare. New York was only a thirty-minute ride from Jersey City, but she was scared.

She didn't want to take the seat next to the fat man in the front, and the only other one vacant was next to the blond guy. He moved his guitar off the seat so she could sit down, although she was so small she could have squeezed in beside it. When she had trouble lifting her duffel bag, he stood up and put it on the overhead rack for her.

The bus lurched and swerved its way up the boulevard and their shoulders touched, a time or two more than they had to. She wanted to lean away, but the man in the seat across the aisle had lit a cigarette and he reeked of smoke and aftershave. "You okay?" the blond asked her. She nodded. He slipped a bottle of soda out of one of his coat pockets and offered her some. She took it, grateful.

"Where you headed?" he said.

"New York."

He smiled, and Keira remembered the bus was a New York express. "Me too," he said. "I have an audition."

"Really?" She felt better hearing this, like she was in the right place.

"A guy I know—he has this band starting up—and they lost their bass player. That's what I play." He tapped the guitar case between his knees. "What about you?"

"I'm going to study ballet. I mean I already do, but I want to get into a better school. My dance teacher studied at Martha Graham." Keira hoped that mentioning Miss Mullen's name would get her in the door there, although she wondered what they'd think if they knew Miss Mullen drank now in the afternoons.

"Graham," he nodded. "That's the big time."

"I'm not sure yet what's involved in getting in. I might try out for the Rockettes in the meantime. Just to make some money."

"Radio City? Cool. You have an audition set up?"

"Not yet." She wasn't sure when the tryouts were.

The blond nodded, offered his hand. "I'm Owen."

"I'm Keira." She extended her hand and wondered if he was holding it too long. Every move he made was making her jittery.

Owen was a talker, but that was fine with her. She looked him over, without making it obvious. He had a scar above his eye that made a space in his eyebrow and she wanted to touch it. "How did you get that scar?" she said.

He grinned. "I can't always get out of my old man's way." He didn't say any more and Keira didn't ask, didn't want to hear about another dad who didn't know how to be one. She leaned back, thought about New York. For almost two years, she'd been saving money in an old shoulder bag her sister Mary didn't want anymore, money she got from babysitting and doing chores for old Mrs. Robinson and her cronies on the block. She pictured herself working in a department store or a coffee shop in midtown, if she had to, someplace where working people would come in for lunch, but of course everyone would know she was really a dancer, busy with rehearsals and auditions, studying with a great teacher. Those things happened in New York.

The light in the bus changed as they entered the Lincoln Tunnel. Keira thought Owen looked handsome in that light. "Are you coming back to New Jersey tonight?" he said.

She swallowed hard, uncertain whether or not to tell him. "I'm never coming back," she said. She'd lain awake the night before, thinking about things she would miss, people she didn't want to be without. She liked the smell of her brother's aftershave when he left the bathroom and the way Mr. Margolis started history class with a joke, because then she got to hear Daryl's laugh. Daryl was big and black and the best player on the basketball team. He moved like a dancer. She would miss watching him play. She would not miss her mother, her rigid distractions that kept her from making any real change in their lives, her inexhaustible excuses for a husband who shamed everything he touched.

"So you have a place lined up to stay?" said Owen.

"Not yet."

He seemed surprised at this. "Have you got a piece of paper?" She didn't. He reached into his pocket and came up with a pack of Winstons. Only one was left and he tucked it behind his ear. Then he removed the shiny silver paper that lined the pack and wrote an address and phone number down. "Listen, here's where I'll be. It's downtown, on Barrow St., near Hudson." Keira didn't understand. "In case you have trouble finding a place." He held out the silver paper and it caught the light and sparkled under the little reading bulb above them.

She took the paper, wondering if this was how he picked up girls. She thanked him for the address, but didn't think she'd need it. "My friend told me about a hostel, not that far from Port Authority." Miss Mullen had told her that dancers took care of each other. They'd share their last cracker.

People were getting up now, putting their coats on. Owen stayed with her till they got outside the Port Authority building, onto Eighth Avenue. He waved as the crowd took her in, and she hurried along with it, felt important. Her bag got heavy in just a few blocks and she stopped to rest every now and then. Stores were opening; people waved down big yellow taxis that bullied their way to the curb.

On a corner near a department store, she stopped to listen to a fiddler playing the music her grandmother liked. The sounds seemed out of place, as did he, but if there were rules about doing this in the street, no one seemed to care. Now and then someone would even put coins in his fiddle case. He wore a Yankees cap and a long, dark overcoat and when he saw Keira watching him, he nodded, began a new tune. She knew this one; it made her want to dance the way her grandmother taught her. Why not, she thought. So she did. With her arms straight down at her sides, she moved out in front of the fiddler and did her step dance. He played with more gusto now, and she added a flourish or two as her long hair bounced and passersby began to gather around them.

When the tune was over, people put more coins and bills into the case. The fiddler asked Keira her name. He had bloodshot eyes, like he hadn't slept, hadn't shaved, and a red mark on his chin from the fiddle. He looked old and he didn't smell so good, like when her father returned from being away several days.

"I'm Keira," she said.

"Well, you're quite a dancer, Keira." He had an accent like her grandmother's and said his name was Samson.

"Really?"

"Yup. I don't believe in stage names. And I don't need no stage."

Keira laughed, but she wondered if all Irishmen thought they could ignore the rules. This one, at least, like her father, seemed indifferent to anything others valued. He asked her if she wanted to dance again, but it sounded more like a demand than a request.

"I can't. I have to be somewhere."

"A pity. Look at the money you've earned us," he said, pointing at the fiddle case. She saw the dollars, but she wanted to get over to Radio City, see when the tryouts were scheduled. "Well, pleasure meeting you." He tipped his hat.

"Yes," she said and turned to get her shoulder bag, but it wasn't there. "My bag. It's gone."

"There's your bag," he said, pointing to her duffel bag.

"No, my shoulder bag. It was right there."

Samson looked up and down the street. Keira looked as well. But they saw no one with her bag. "It's no good leaving a purse unattended on the street," he said.

"My money was in it. What am I going to do?"

"Dance with me here and I'll give you half of whatever we get."

Keira looked away so he wouldn't see how close to tears she was. If she danced all day, she'd never replace the money she'd saved. Samson began something slow and melancholy, then picked up the pace, as if to coax her, and she began. The circle changed with each tune, faces became new faces, different smiles. Keira danced for a very long time. She avoided looking at anyone, focused on the bikes whizzing by, the busses hissing and heaving their way up the street. Everything moved with her, keeping time. Sometimes she went so fast, the little crowd would cheer or clap their hands. Now and then someone would join her, lifting their knees, holding a hat in the air.

The morning light changed, turned harsher, reflecting off surfaces she hadn't noticed before. Her head was light, her legs heavy. Someone behind her was calling to her. No, jeering. She didn't want to turn, but she couldn't help herself. Three teen-age boys stood outside the circle, heckling. Their antics made a few people laugh. She lost her footing. No one had ever mocked her dancing before. No one. At home, at school, at the dance studio, Keira had come to take compliments as her due.

She missed another step, stumbled. Samson slowed down, and she walked toward him, head down. The boys got bored and moved along. The people left.

"You did good," Samson said. But Keira didn't think so. The laughter had shaken her. She couldn't imagine what she'd been thinking to come to a city like New York and expect to dance. What a fool she was.

Samson tucked his fiddle between his legs, stretched his arms. "You wore me out. How much we got?" he said.

Keira squatted beside the case. Bills were inside and more had fallen nearby. She gathered only the paper money and stood up to count it. "Eighteen dollars," she told him.

"Take nine for yourself."

She noticed he didn't offer to share the coins.

"Thanks," she said and began to count off her share.

"Just leave a single in the case."

"Why?"

"Power of suggestion." He knelt, placed the fiddle down gently and gathered the coins into a small pouch.

"Thank you," Keira said.

He looked up, smiling, as if he knew something about her she didn't understand yet. "It was a pleasure. I hope you'll come back."

I may have to, she thought, and nodded.

"Good luck to you then," he said.

At Forty-sixth Street she headed toward Sixth Avenue. The lights of the marquees were still out, as if the theaters were sleeping late. The marquee for Radio City was huge, curving around the corner of the building, lit in red and blue, but the theatre itself was dark. She walked up to a set of glass doors. Inside, a man was sweeping. He looked up from his work and she waived, tried to open the door, but it was locked. He came over and opened it a crack. "Theatre is closed," he grumbled. He was old with very dark skin and very white hair.

"Yes, I know. I was wondering about the Rockettes."

"Like I said, theatre is closed."

"Do you know where they hold their tryouts?"

"Don't know anything about that. Anyway, the theatre is closed." He pulled the door shut and stepped away.

Keira pounded on the glass.

He returned, irritated.

"Do you know how I can find out?" she said.

"Look what you're doing to the glass. I just cleaned those doors."

Couldn't he just answer a simple question? "I'm trying to find out about the auditions."

"For Chrissake," he muttered, opening the door to let her in. "Wait here. Maybe there's something in the office." He disappeared through a door a few steps away.

Keira had been to Radio City only once before, when her father had taken her and Mary to the Christmas show. The lobby was just as magnificent as she remembered, with its huge chandelier and the wide staircase that led to a landing with a beautiful mural. But without the crowds, without the anticipation of a show about to begin, the air still, it felt more like a church now, like a sacred place that would receive her prayer, welcome it even, if she offered it with the reverence that a great theater like this deserved. And so she did. She prayed that one day she would dance in New York.

The old man returned, handed her a flyer, and shooed her out the door. She leaned against a car to read it. The first requirement listed was age. You had to be eighteen, and you had to prove it. Keira felt as if she'd been accused of something she hadn't done. What difference did a year and a half make anyway? She was just as good a dancer now as she would be then, just as ready to learn, and what clutz couldn't kick her legs in the air. Maybe she could use Mary's birth certificate. Mary wouldn't care. She could send it in the mail. She wondered if the hostel let you receive mail.

If she had to, she'd wait it out. That's all. She'd find another way to make money, get a place to live. There were a million stores in this area. One of them had to need a salesgirl or a stock clerk. She headed back the way she came. The streets were crowded now, noisy. At the corner someone rushing to cross the street jostled her as the light was changing. She looked for the fiddler, but he was gone. Her stomach felt the way it did when her father left them on their own, when she couldn't imagine how her mother would find the money to buy food or pay the rent.

Near one of the theatres, a woman sat in a doorway, her legs stretched out in front of her. She wore knee-high white boots and her bare thighs showed below a short black skirt. Her hair was wild and thick and the color of a fire truck. Keira got closer, tried not to stare. The woman lifted her chin and let out a stream of cigarette smoke, gave Keira a nod that was more like a dare than a greeting. Keira stopped, nodded back, although she wasn't sure that's what was wanted.

"You home on leave," the woman said, pointing to the duffle bag at Keira's feet.

She was very young, maybe even a teenager. Her elaborate eye makeup reminded Keira of when she'd played dress-up with Mary, raiding their mother's cosmetic case. It dawned on her then what this girl was, but she'd imagined prostitutes were older, not as pretty.

"I'm from New Jersey." Keira looked over her shoulder, wondering if she should just move on.

"Don't be so quick to admit that," the girl chuckled, exhaling again. Her lipstick left a bright red ring on the filter. "I'm from the great state of Texas." She had an accent.

"Really?"

"Except my part of it wasn't so great." The girl pulled in her long legs and sprang up to her full height, almost as tall as Keira. "I'm Dee Dee," she said and flicked her cigarette butt to the curb.

Keira didn't offer her hand, didn't want to touch her.

"You hungry?" the girl said.

Keira didn't know what to make of the sudden invitation, but she hadn't eaten all morning. "Yeah," she said.

"Let's go get something."

"Okay."

Dee Dee sized her up, seemed to be deciding something. "You got any money?"

"I have some. Yes," Keira said. Immediately, she wondered if that was the right thing to say.

They crossed the street to a coffee shop, and Dee Dee got an unpleasant look from the man behind the counter. He was short with a very dark, thick mustache that quivered with annoyance. "Don't worry, Nick," she told him. "I ain't staying long. She led the way to a table in the back and the waitress who brought their menus wasn't happy to see her either. She tossed them down and left without a greeting. "Bitch is always on the rag," mumbled Dee Dee.

"Why do you come here?" Keira whispered. "They don't seem very friendly."

"I'm fussy about my eggs," she said, and studied the menu.

"God, I'm starving."

"Have whatever you want," Dee Dee told her. "The hospitality sucks, but the grub is good and the price is right."

They both ordered pancakes; only Dee Dee wanted coffee and bacon. She lit a cigarette and held it between her lips while she wiggled out of her jacket. Her sweater had a deep scoop neckline trimmed with little blue rhinestones. Her breasts were big and pushed up. "So you ain't in school?" Dee Dee said, squinting through the smoke.

"Not today."

"Field trip?"

"Sort of," said Keira. She wasn't sure how much she should tell this girl. "I'm planning to live here. I'm a dancer."

"There's no smoking in here," Nick yelled to them. "No smoking."

"Asshole," Dee Dee mumbled, crushing the cigarette under her heel. "So what's the problem?" she said to Keira. "People don't dance in New Jersey?"

"All the serious dancers are here in New York."

Dee Dee laughed hard, made Keira wish she hadn't said that. The girl moved the sugar and ketchup aside, as if they were blocking what she had to say. "Really appreciate you springing for breakfast like this. I'm a little short."

Keira wasn't surprised at this. "It's okay. I earned some money today."

"Earned how?" said Dee Dee, with a look that made Keira uncomfortable.

"Dancing. With a guy who plays the fiddle."

Dee Dee seemed relieved at this.

"My shoulder bag was stolen. So he let me dance for a while and gave me some of the money we earned."

"So you need money?"

"Yeah."

"You ain't gonna make it dancing for dimes."

"I'm going to find a job in a department store."

"Good luck with that. You know how many people in this town are looking for work?"

Keira wouldn't admit to the possibility of not finding a job, but failure now didn't seem as remote as it had this morning.

"You got looks. You could make some real money if you wanted." Dee Dee sounded like she was bragging. Keira looked down at the table; she didn't want to hear how Dee Dee earned her money.

"You don't need to put your nose up. It ain't what you think."

"I don't think anything. Honest." Keira wished Dee Dee would just drop the subject.

But she kept at it. "There's other stuff you can do, you know. You could make bundles and still wear a white dress down the aisle. All you have to do is open your mouth, for Chrissake."

Keira pictured what she meant, and her heart raced from the shock of it. Dee Dee made it sound like a service, like cutting someone's hair.

The waitress brought their pancakes and Dee Dee patted the woman's behind. "Good job, Doris." The waitress's surly response didn't bother her. Dee Dee told her to bring more syrup and more coffee and another juice for Keira. She was like someone on a holiday. "Are you sure you don't want some bacon?" she said, her mouth full.

"Thanks, no," Keira said.

"Try the jam. It's great." Then she went on about all the money she'd be collecting at the end of the day, and Keira wondered why she couldn't afford to buy her own breakfast. "Trouble is I'm a big spender. See these boots?" She stretched out her leg to show off the shiny white leather. "A hundred bucks."

Keira couldn't taste her food, couldn't eat. She thought about the money it would take for the kind of ballet slippers she should have, the cost of lessons at a school like Martha Graham's and how long it was going to take to make it all happen.

"Can't you get diseases doing that?" Keira kept her voice low.

"Don't believe everything the nuns tell you," Dee Dee said. "There's more to worry about on the toilet seats in this town." Keira didn't believe it could really be that easy, and Dee Dee read her look. "You just have to make up your mind what you're willing to do."

Keira wanted to ask what things she meant exactly. Maybe she wasn't talking about anything that would really be that bad, but Dee Dee wasn't looking at her anymore. She was looking at the entrance and she seemed uneasy. Keira turned. A man in a long expensive-looking overcoat had come in. He didn't greet Nick. He just walked with slow, hammering steps toward their table. In a breath, he was beside them, leaning over, with his face in Dee Dee's face. He didn't look angry, but he seemed like someone who could do great harm. "I thought I told you I didn't want you in here," he said. His voice sounded oiled.

"Fuck off," Dee Dee told him, but she scratched the side of her neck nervously.

The man laughed, lifted his wrist to look at his shiny watch. "Time's a wastin', girl."

"I ain't wasting time. I'm talking to Keira here. She's interested in working for you." The man looked from one to the other, deciding whether to believe her. "It's the truth."

Keira felt lightheaded. She saw the toe shoes, shoes with proper padding, trimmed in silk. She saw herself tying the long ribbons around her ankles.

"Is that so?" the man said. The words slid out, coated and slimy.

Keira was too nervous to speak.

"She's going to need training wheels," Dee Dee told him. "But that's no problem. Right, Len?" Keira caught Dee Dee's look, the dare in it, noticed the man's gold cufflinks.

"We'll talk later on," he said and put a hand on Dee Dee's shoulder. But there was no affection in it, only ownership. "Four o'clock. Same address as yesterday," he said, in the same greasy tone. "And pick me up some cigarettes when you're finished." He threw a twenty-dollar bill on the table in front of her and left.

"That's Len," Dee Dee said when the door closed behind him. "He takes care of things." Her cheeks were flushed, but she spoke as if he'd done nothing out of the ordinary. "So you planning on sticking around?"

"I don't know," Keira said. She felt sick. The man had left something unsavory behind. The air seemed heavier, like when her father was in one of his moods, and her food tasted like ashes now.

Dee Dee shrugged. "What are you going to do? Go home to Mommy?"

"I can go home if I want."

"Well, you better do it soon. You think your family's going to welcome you back once you run out of luck? When you fuck up so bad they don't want you around? It don't work like that."

Keira stood up, tipping over the chair. She righted it, put her jacket on.

"Yeah, me too. I gotta go," Dee Dee said, striding toward the door.

Keira gathered her things and paid the check. When she got outside, Dee Dee was waiting. It seemed colder than before, and Keira wasn't sure what to do. She looked at the girl, the silly makeup, the phony hair color. Yet she seemed so sure of herself. Keira didn't know whether to run or beg her to take her along.

The girl waited for Keira to say something, but she didn't. "Maybe I'll see you around," Dee Dee said.

"Yeah," Keira said.

Dee Dee ambled into the street on her high-heeled boots, not waiting for the light to turn green. Keira watched her for a while, but soon people and passing cars blocked the way and she could see only flashes of sun in her burning red hair.

Keira walked several blocks before she realized that she was headed toward the Port Authority. It wasn't a decision. It was a reflex. She wanted to be some place safe, even if that meant going home. She was afraid here, afraid of what she might do.

The depot was more crowded than it had been in the morning, and she wasn't sure which platform the bus left from. She asked a woman in uniform, who told her it was leaving right away and if she hurried she could make it. She moved as quickly as she could and the pounding rhythm of her steps put a tune into her head, one the fiddler had played. She couldn't get rid of it.

When she reached the platform, she took her place in the slow-moving line of slouching people waiting to board the bus. She could feel the heat from inside the door as she stepped high to get in, smell how close it was going to feel in there. She looked down the aisle, saw the people settling back in their seats, closing their eyes, relieved to be finished with the city, leaving it behind.

A man excused himself to get around her and into the aisle. He wore an overcoat that smelled musty, as if it had just been taken out from a long stay in the back of a closet. Her best hiding place had been the closet. Under the bed was no good; you could still hear the cries, the sound of fists on flesh. The closet had a door you could close and in the near silence, she could repeat the words to herself—*plié, relevé, sauté*—in a place so dark she didn't even have to close her eyes to imagine the people looking up at her from the front row.

The bus driver wasn't looking at her, didn't notice the little stir she made as she turned without warning, bumping her bag into the man behind her as she jumped back down off the bus. "I'm sorry," she told him. "I don't want to go."

The man laughed, his belly bouncing inside his tight jacket. "Then I guess you shouldn't," he said.

Outside, on Eighth Avenue, people coming out of the Port Authority fanned out in every direction. Traffic crawled along, and the sunlight glinted off the windshields of cars passing through the intersection. Everyone hurried along, no matter how loudly the billboards and storefront signs insisted on being noticed. Keira fell in behind two men with briefcases, not sure if she was headed uptown or down. She tried to remember the street she was on when she met Dee Dee, which direction the girl had taken.

After a block, she saw she was headed uptown. She quickened her pace but paused when she spotted a poster for the Joffrey pasted on the fence of a construction site. She knew she didn't have enough money to buy a ticket. She wasn't even sure she had enough to get something to eat, and she wondered how long it would take to find Dee Dee. She dug into the pocket of her jeans to see how much she had left. It was the wrong pocket and she found only a single piece of paper that didn't feel like money. A breeze took the paper out of her hand and it skittered a few yards ahead of her until it lodged itself in a nest of debris where the construction fence met a wall. Keira didn't give it much thought, not until she got closer and saw it sparkling in the sunlight, like Christmas tinsel. She picked it up, turned it over, remembering the back of his freckled hand, and saw she was going the wrong way.

HERE AND NOW

The baseball field near Terry's high school is eight blocks from the house, at the end of a dirt road that winds along sandy patches of tall weeds and skinny trees so frail even the birds don't bother with them. It doesn't usually take her long to walk there, but today she has Grandma Hilda with her and the old woman has been getting distracted, stopping to greet dog walkers, admire lawns that have defied the drought.

"Hilda, come on," she says. Terry has been calling her grandmother by her first name since kindergarten. She remembers her mother scolding her for it, but Hilda never seemed to mind. "The game's started already," she calls, but Hilda doesn't come. She bends down to peer at something near the fence.

By the time Hilda and Terry reach the field, Terry is sweaty and uncomfortable. The huge black-topped parking lot is way too large and way too far from the bleachers, especially on a hot day like this one. There's no escaping the sun. The refreshment stand, rarely open, has a narrow overhang that offers about as much shade as a postcard. The metal bleachers get hot enough to bake thighs. Nobody over forty lasts more than an inning without a towel to sit on, so Terry has beach chairs. They're not heavy, but after eight blocks, they're irritating her shoulder and scratching the side of her leg.

Terry's a sophomore now. She's been living with Hilda for five years, ever since her parents separated. She saw them a lot in the beginning, but that didn't last. Her father left their unremarkable New Jersey shore town and moved to Greenwich, Connecticut, with his fancy new wife and their flawless new baby. After a while he treated Terry like an old car—you keep it cause it still runs, maybe take it for a spin once in a while, but the new model is the one you take care of, the one you want the neighbors to notice.

Terry's mother, Greta, weary from years of commuting to the city and decades of living in hiding, had long since made plans to move to Manhattan. She'd lived in Atlantic Hills all her life, hated it. The town has zero personality, she says, no bookshops, no arts community, nothing to make anyone want to stick around—except maybe the view of Manhattan. She's far from wrong, although Hilda would never admit it. On weekends, parents numb out at their kids' soccer games. When there's no game, they go to the mall and shop themselves silly. The ones who insist on having a purpose in life go to Home Depot. And if there are others like Greta, who've fallen into the deathly pattern of posing as a loving wife, a woman who doesn't desire other women, they keep it to themselves.

Hilda, baffled by her daughter's revelation but saddened by her pain, understood she had to leave. She found a place on the Upper West Side. That's where Terry was supposed to go, until she and Hilda finally convinced Greta to let her stay in Atlantic Hills, at least until the end of the school year. Hilda's house was just a few blocks from the school, and it would be easy for Greta to visit.

Hilda hired a full-time helper, a retired nurse's aide named Margaret, who lived across the street. The woman did a bit of laundry, a bit of cooking, occasional dusting, but mainly she was there to keep Greta from arguing that Terry was a burden on Hilda. She wasn't. She and Hilda were a perfect fit, always had been. They'd bonded for keeps before Terry was a month old, when Greta's maternity leave ended and Hilda filled in.

The school year ended without incident and so did the summer and by the start of sixth grade the notion of Terry moving to the city became something no longer discussed. Greta's resentment about it would surface now and then, but Terry sensed the relief as well. Her mother got promoted, took on more clients, and her visits, frequent enough at first, trailed off. Terry was safe, doing well in school—even better than before the separation—and the friends she'd made in preschool became a tight knit group.

•

Terry reaches the gate that opens to the field and calls to Hilda again, with no effect. She lifts her hair off her neck, but it brings no relief, because it's not just the heat that's getting to her. It's Hilda. She's not herself anymore, not all the time, not for almost a year now. She forgets things, some important, some not—whether she took her medicine or paid the gas bill, the neighbor's name. So Terry keeps a close eye on her, does everything she can to cover for her, but people are starting to notice the lapses. Margaret stays past seven most nights, to keep Hilda company while Terry gets her homework done. Terry's boyfriend, Danny, is worried. He scolds Terry for keeping the worst of it from her mother. But she resists telling Greta too much, because she's bound to overreact. Then how long would it be before she decides Terry can't stay with Hilda anymore and moves her to New York, away from her school, her friends, everything she cares about?

Hilda finally catches up, and they head through the gate toward the bleachers. A bunch of people, maybe ten or so, probably parents with the visiting team, are sitting shoulder to shoulder in the highest row. The section reserved for Terry's school has a scattering of parents, along with a few seniors from the football team.

Terry sets up the chairs at the far end of the home-team bleachers, just behind first base. The bottom of the second inning is already under way. No score yet, but Atlantic Regional has men on first and second. Hilda wants to know about the batter—his name, what year he's in, what position he plays—so Terry fills her in. Danny is on base, and Hilda claps her hands, delighted with him.

By the end of the third inning, more kids from school have arrived—all freshmen—and they've laid claim to the top row of the home-team bleachers. Every now and then one of the boys shouts out the name of a player he knows, offering support, but most of their energy is spent razzing the visiting team.

Hilda's questions have trailed off but she remains attentive, until she notices crazy Mary, the disheveled old woman Terry and her friends see around town now and then, especially when the weather turns mild. She wears long dresses with ragged hemlines that reach below her calves and a dirty raincoat just as long. Her swollen veiny ankles are stuffed like sausages into ratty sneakers that must have been white at one time, and she pushes a shopping cart overflowing with a bizarre assortment of her precious junk. She talks nonstop but has no phone on her as far as Terry can tell. Sometimes she sounds almost conversational, as if she's filling the world in on her family's comings and goings. Other times she seems frightened, angry even, that people don't see what's happening all around them. That's actually when she makes the most sense to Terry, when she's wailing about children being shot at their desks or faucets spouting poisoned water.

Hilda leans forward in her chair to get a better look at the woman. She's seen her around often enough before so Terry can't understand why she's so fascinated with her now. She taps Hilda's shoulder to distract her, points to the boy at bat. "Look. It's Josephine's brother. He didn't think he'd get in the game today." It doesn't work. Hilda raises her arm, her plaid carry-all swinging from her elbow, and waves to crazy Mary, calling her over. Terry begs her to stop, tugs at her arm. She's afraid Danny will see Hilda acting weird. But Mary is already navigating the bumpy path between them, guiding her cart, a stuffed parakeet wedged into the front, like a hood ornament on an old Chevy. Hilda beckons Mary closer, as if she's been saving her a choice seat.

"Stop that," Terry tells her. "We don't want her sitting with us."

Hilda glares at her. "That's very unkind of you," she says. "Very unkind."

Mary is just a step or two away now and Terry can smell her, a dreadful odor like something rotting in a damp basement. "I have it. I had it all along," the woman tells them, as if this is news they've been waiting to hear.

"I'm so glad," Hilda answers, sounding relieved.

"They told me I wouldn't need it," Mary says, "but I don't listen to them anymore. I don't listen."

Terry groans. God knows what wavelength these two are on. Terry usually manages to cover up for Hilda when she starts acting strange. Weeks go by when Hilda is her old self again, long stretches when she's as sharp and perceptive as ever. Even Margaret says so. But Danny has known Hilda too long, since before Terry started high school. He's hard to fool.

So is Greta. Last month, at the end of one of her rare visits, she leaned into the hallway mirror to apply a parting coat of lipstick and whispered that it might be time to find a safer place for Hilda. Terry wanted to smack the tube out of her hand. "She's safe right here, with me," she said, unable to soften her tone.

Greta didn't contradict her. She didn't have to. "We'll see how it goes," she said. "But we should get things settled before school starts next year."

"She's fine, Mom. Ask Margaret. She's here all day with her."

"I talked to Margaret. She's taking Grandma to the doctor next week." Her voice was flat, quietly firm, the way she speaks to subordinates when she's past the point of compromise. Terry heard the edge in it and wondered if her mother wasn't somehow satisfied that Terry's years of resistance to moving to the city might turn out pointless after all.

Mary rummages through her cart, comes up with a frying pan that's missing its handle.

Hilda reaches for the beat-up pan. "Will we need this?" she says.

"Don't touch that. It's dirty," Terry says, careful to keep her voice down, because they're attracting attention.

Hilda takes the pan anyway, turning it this way and that. "Where's the handle?" she says, unfazed by the grease stains scorched into it.

"Grandma, give that back."

"He broke it," Mary says. "I knew he'd break it. I warned him." Her voice is loud and abrasive, out of sync with the cheers and prompts of the little crowd and the indistinct voices from the dugouts. Terry can't see a way to get rid of her.

"You gonna fry up some burgers?" one of the freshmen calls. His crowd rewards him with a chorus of nasty laughter.

Mary raises a fist and yells up at the boy. "You broke it!"

The kids wave their arms, gleeful they've engaged her. "Make mine with cheese," someone yells. More chime in, shouting over each other like impatient waiters to a short-order cook. Mary fidgets, her shoulders rising and falling in a jerky rhythm, unnerved by their relentless jibes. She takes back the pan, grabs the handle of her cart, and pushes her belongings across the length of the bleachers, back toward the gate.

The boys have upset Hilda as well and she turns to Terry, as if there's something they should do to stop them. Terry shakes her head to show she disapproves, secretly grateful that the teasing made Mary retreat. She doesn't want Hilda to have an *incident*. That's the word

Terry uses now for the more serious lapses. They're not like the little missteps that began last summer, easy to dismiss. These are bigger, stranger, impossible to mistake as anything but the terrifying signs of something going very wrong.

Like the one two months ago, early in the morning. Terry's dog, Slug, a cross-eyed border collie, led the way into the sewing room. He sat at attention beside Hilda's chair, tail dusting the floor, as if expecting a reward for getting Terry out of bed. Hilda was bent over her old Singer. It was odd for her to be sewing at that hour, but the machine's steady purr was the sound of Hilda at her best—capable, attentive—and Terry tried not to worry. "How come you're at the machine already?"

Hilda straightened up, the back of her sewing chair higher than her head. Her hair, mostly white and long, way past her shoulders, was pinned up as usual, a filigreed halo against the blue upholstery. She smiled, a cure-all, and Terry came and stood behind her chair, kneading her shoulders. She smelled like minty toothpaste. "I'll have this finished today," Hilda said. She was making Terry a jacket to wear over her dress for the spring dance.

"What's the rush?" Terry said. The dance was still weeks away, and the jacket looked to Terry as if it was coming along nicely. She didn't want a new jacket anyway, though she didn't have the heart to tell Hilda that. She'd found one in the attic, a relic of Hilda's, with shoulder pads and tiny pearl buttons and cuffed sleeves. With a few alterations, it would be so perfectly retro. They used to do that together, rework the gems Terry dug out of dusty trunks. Awesome stuff. Double-breasted suits and bell-bottom pants, mini-dresses with geometric patterns of bright circles and squares.

"I think we're just about done here," Hilda said, lifting the jacket with a flourish.

"You finished the sleeves already?"

"Last night. Just had to add the piping. You should try it on. That way I can press it while you're in school."

Hilda pushed her chair back and stood to hold up the jacket. Terry slipped an arm into one of the sleeves, and the lining felt silky. But when she tried to get her hand into the other sleeve, she couldn't find the opening. She twisted around to see if Hilda might be holding the jacket at the wrong angle, but that wasn't it. The opening at the shoulder was too small, smaller than her fist.

Terry pulled off the jacket and spread it open on the loveseat. "I think something went wrong. Here. See?" Slug stepped up as if to have a look for himself.

Hilda leaned over to examine the sleeve. "Yes, I see what happened." Color rose in her cheeks, and she sounded hoarse. "I can fix it," she insisted, but she seemed uncertain, her chin trembling.

Terry put her arm around her. "No, leave it," she said, folding the jacket over her arm. She hated seeing Hilda upset like this. "I'll wear my black jacket, the one you made me last year. I love that one."

Hilda snatched the garment away. "No. You'll have a new jacket, as we planned." The dog slunk out of the room, tail down, as if fearing he'd be blamed. "I can fix this," she repeated harshly. But Terry wondered who she was really trying to convince. She seemed to be talking to herself. This was one of the girl's first encounters with it—Hilda's new alien, unpredictable self, bent on betraying her.

The incidents, big and small, are more frequent now, and Terry hates them. Hilda sometimes calls her Greta. She doesn't correct her, but she wants her grandmother the way she used to be. She knew the fabrics Terry loved, the snacks she couldn't pass up, the names of her friends. She kept track of Terry's doctors' appointments, her vaccinations, her shoe sizes, her height each year since the first time she stood up on her own.

The girl spoke her first words to her grandmother, and later her schoolgirl secrets. They became confidantes, a connection Terry never had with her mother, whose long silences and dark moods left the girl feeling she'd caused them. Hilda's house, just blocks from the beach, was a wonderland for Terry. When they played hospital together, she would be Dr. Terry and Grandma would be ailing Hilda, the patient she miraculously cured—over and over and over again. It took every instrument in the doctor's kit to get her well, and Terry had a merciless array of plastic needles and nasty little sugar pills, but Hilda endured them without complaint, as if the child was destined to free mankind from every ill.

Terry resents the meanness of what's happening, how spiteful life can be. Gratitude doesn't come easily anymore, because she has no time for it. More and more, the details of their day, even paying the bills and making dinner, are left to her.

Sometimes when she's in class or standing at her locker, her mind is at home, following her grandmother from one room to another, praying she won't leave a hot iron on a blouse or forget she has something in the oven. Between classes she calls Margaret to check in. When Terry was little, she used to follow Hilda from room to room. The woman couldn't leave her chair without Terry chasing after her. It was like a game, because wherever Hilda went, she'd find something to show the child—a string of beads, a huge wooden spoon. And no matter what it was, Hilda could transform it. A handkerchief became an exotic veil. The buttons in her sewing box turned into Roman coins. And Hilda would let her take the treasures home if she wanted to. But Terry didn't want that. She wanted all those magical things to stay where they were, in Hilda's house, so she could find them again the next time. Years later, after her parents had gone their separate ways, Terry understood that the only magic had been Hilda, and the way the woman loved her.

•

The freshmen cup their mouths and shout louder, some of them stomping on the metal bleachers. "Hey, Mary," one boy calls, "you can't leave. I'm hungry."

"Where is she going?" Hilda says, getting to her feet. She waves her hand in the air to get Mary's attention and tips over her chair.

"Hilda, stop."

"Come back," Hilda calls. "Come back."

"Sit down. Please," Terry tells her, righting the chair.

Hilda sits, but she's gesturing with both hands now, like a refugee parted from her child.

"Where's my burger?" a boy yells, waving a dollar bill in the air.

"That's enough out of you," shouts one of the fathers. It's Mr. Lynch, Danny's dad. The boys get quiet but not for long, because Mary lets out an anguished string of curses as she searches her cart, lamenting the loss of some possession.

A line drive to center field takes the attention off Mary. But the ball smacks into the outfielder's glove, ending the suspense, and the boys start in on her again, calling, whistling, hooting. One throws an empty soda can, and Mr. Lynch stands, points a finger at one of the freshmen. "Are you gonna knock it off? Or do I have to come up there?" he says, climbing two rows closer to where they're seated, daring them to step up. No one volunteers.

Hilda can't settle down. She's mumbling things Terry can't make out. She whispers gently that it's time to go, but Hilda resists, her eyes glued on Mary. Arched over the cart, the woman removes random items one by one—a small vase, a metal ashtray, a can of Campbell's soup—and places them on the ground.

Terry stands up. "Come on. Let's go home."

She won't move.

"I have it," Mary calls to them. With a bright yellow, floppy-brimmed sun hat retrieved from her cart, she heads toward them again, holding it up like a salesclerk ready to show them the perfect gift. "I have it," she repeats, "I have it," as if Hilda's been waiting far too long for this gem. She shuffles closer, crossing the length of the bleachers, her voice loud and nasal, but there's a kind of confidence in it, as if she understands something about Hilda that Terry can't.

"I don't feel good. Please," Terry whispers. "We have to leave." She wants to wrench her out of the chair, end this fiasco. But Hilda won't listen and Terry wants to shake her. She wants her life back. She wants Hilda out of her head, out of her plans just for one damn day. Nothing is the same anymore. Nothing can happen that isn't about Hilda. They can't even watch television in peace. The other night she wandered out of the living room, out of the house. Terry thought she'd gone to the kitchen until Slug spotted her outside, barefoot on the lawn, and scratched at the screen door to get to her. Terry pulled her back inside, screaming at her, picturing what might have happened had she wandered down the road, onto the highway.

Hilda was shaken, both of them in tears. Terry apologized, made her some tea, but she couldn't sleep that night. The familiar panic settled icy on her skin, the dread that Hilda can't be fixed, that life will be turned inside out again, like when her parents split up. Terry turned on her side, pulled the quilt to her chin, let the warmth erase the fear. Hilda will be all right. The bad spells come and go and she always comes around.

Hilda looks up at her granddaughter, a familiar flash of concern on her face. "What's wrong? Are you getting your period?" She says it loud enough to draw giggles from some boys nearby. Terry puts a finger to her lips, desperate to quiet her. At first, when her grandmother couldn't finish a sentence or forgot to turn the car off or pay the phone bill, Terry mostly felt sorry for her, a little worried. Now it's not so simple, because the anger sets in. It's like something caught in her throat, something she can't swallow. She knows it's wrong. She loves Hilda and she loves living at her house. Being there after her parents broke up helped her pretend her parents were still just a few blocks away. One of them might walk through Hilda's door at any moment and ask to see her homework or take her to the mall. But by the time she started high school, she stopped pretending. She tried not to need them as much because there was no point. Nothing she did ever made them change. She clung to her friends, to Danny, and in Hilda's house that sense she'd always had of being in the way was gone.

Hilda finally rises from the chair, but Mary is on them, pressing the sun hat into Hilda's hand, talking nonsense. The freshmen make the most of it, taunting and laughing, but they stop abruptly when Lynch scolds them again. Other parents join in, telling the boys they'll have them barred from the games. Hilda, upset, lets the sun hat drop to the ground.

Terry feels a hand on her shoulder. It's Danny. "It's okay," he tells Hilda, his tone measured, the way he'd talk to a frazzled pitcher. Hilda gets up, takes his arm, lets him lead her toward the gate. Terry's not surprised. Hilda is always calmer when Danny's around. She trusts him. He knows how to get her to smile. He makes everybody smile. That's what made Terry like him so much in the first place, when she found him standing on the beach that day. She was still living with her parents then. Her dad was mostly not around and her mom was forever going on about how Terry would love living in Manhattan.

It was a rainy Saturday morning—after yet another foot-stomping, book-throwing tantrum that did nothing to convince her mother to let her live with Hilda. Terry stormed out of the house and wound up at the beach. And there was Danny, pulling as hard as he could on a fishing line, trying to reel in his catch.

Danny was in seventh grade, two years ahead of her, so she didn't see him every day, but she recognized him right away. His thick curls, wet from the rain, were stuck to his forehead, and he wobbled as the reel resisted him. She watched as he got the fish out of the water, then moved closer till she was an arm's length away.

The fish—a fluke, it turned out—twisted and wiggled in front of him on the line. He tried to reason with the thing, calling it Frankie. She loved the way he talked to it, the way he chuckled. Then she heard a sound she almost didn't recognize—her own laughter.

Danny wanted to throw Frankie back into the water, said his mom was tired of cleaning fish guts every weekend. So Terry took him and Frankie to her grandmother's house. Danny and Hilda cleaned the fish at the kitchen counter, their hands all gushy from fluke innards, their faces contorted into a silly mix of disgust and glee, and Terry knew she could never go to New York with her mom. She could never be anywhere but right here, with them.

Up ahead, Danny and Hilda pass through the gate, but Mary follows them, stopping here and there to pick up the things she placed on the ground. Terry folds up the chairs, grateful they don't weigh much, and hurries past her, but Mary lumbers after. Terry glances back at her, sees her closing the gap, cart in tow, the yellow hat perched on her head. She gives the woman a look meant to discourage, but it doesn't. "Go away," Terry tells her. The urge to cry sneaks up on her. Why can't they do something about these people? How can she be allowed to roam the streets like this?

Danny and Hilda are in the parking lot when Terry catches up. "Those boys are a disgrace," Hilda says.

"I know," Terry agrees, putting the chairs down. She can tell Danny is upset because he won't look at her, even when she touches his arm.

"I've a good mind to call the principal's office." Hilda rummages through her bag. "Terry, did I give you my phone?"

"This is insane," Danny whispers.

"She's always like that," Terry says, looking over at Mary, standing at the far corner of the lot, beside a bin overflowing with donated clothing.

"I don't mean *her*," he says, ushering Terry a few steps away from her grandmother. "I mean Hilda. Look at what's happening to her. Maybe your mother's right. Maybe she needs to be in the city with her?"

"Stop it. She'll hear you."

"How long do you think you can keep this up?"

"Hilda's fine. She just said she wants to call the principal. Does that sound like someone who doesn't understand what's going on?"

"Stop playing games. She's losing it."

"What old person doesn't get weird sometimes? It's not that bad." She watches Mary lift a plastic trash bag left leaning against the bin, and it splits open, its multicolored innards bursting out. "Anyway, Margaret and I watch out for her."

"Did you tell your mother she left the house the other night?"

"She doesn't need to know every little thing. Besides, Hilda understands. We talk about everything. She knows she's forgetting things. She knows we have to be more careful. My mother would only blow it out of proportion." Terry turns, ready to head back to Hilda.

"I'll tell her then."

Terry stops abruptly. "What did you say?" She wants him to repeat it, because she can't believe he understands what he's saying.

"I'm calling her after the game."

Terry moves in close. "This can't be left up to my mother."

"I can't watch this happen to her."

Terry steps away from him, but he grabs her arm. "This is no good. Can't you see that?"

"My mother doesn't care what happens to Hilda," she hisses.

"Of course, she cares. She's your mother."

"She'd undo that if she could. And she won't think twice about turning her back on Hilda, dumping her in some nursing home. Just like she turned her back on everyone else."

"You don't know that. You've got to talk with her."

"And how often do you think you'll see me once I'm stuck in a high rise on the Upper West Side?"

"Don't be so dramatic. Moving to the city isn't the end of the world," Danny tells her. He's graduating in two months, has his own car, thinks the world is his backyard. Even before he got his license, he was driving into Manhattan with his dad. "We could see each other whenever we want."

"And what happens to Hilda?" Terry says.

"She'll love New York. She's always telling me she doesn't get in there enough."

"Mom's place is too small for the three of us."

"So you'll find a bigger place."

Danny doesn't get it. He comes from a home where parents are attentive, loyal. Terry is sure that Greta would never want Hilda in New York, not unless it's in a place for old people and caring for her is somebody else's job.

"You know what living with her would be like? I'd be an afterthought again, an occasional shopping companion, someone who isn't needed by anyone—cause Hilda would be put away."

Hilda calls to Terry again.

"I can take care of my grandmother, so just stay out of it." Terry returns to Hilda's side, tells her Danny needs to get back to the game.

"No," he says, catching up. "I'll walk you home." He picks up the chairs.

"Don't be stupid," Terry says. "You'll wind up on the bench just for leaving the game." She tugs at the chairs, but Danny holds on.

"She's right," Hilda says, patting his arm. "I'll come to the next game. And the playoffs too."

Terry can't help smirking at him. Hilda knows exactly what's going on. She knows where she is. He's all wrong.

"It's not that far," Danny says. "I'm coming with you."

"No, you're not. We're fine."

Terry's tone draws a puzzled glance from Hilda. "You're angry," she says. "What's wrong?"

"I'm not. My stomach's bothering me."

Danny hands her the chairs, and Terry hangs them over one arm. For Hilda's sake she gives him a wave before she coaxes her away from him, as he heads back to the field. She tries to get Hilda to walk faster, because Mary has lost interest in the Goodwill bin and she's headed their way, calling to Hilda, who turns to look at her.

"Look," Mary calls. "Look what I have."

Hilda stops. "She's telling us something."

"Ignore her. She's not talking to us."

"Yes, she is. She's looking right at us."

Terry tugs at Hilda's elbow, but it does no good. "Please. My stomach hurts. I need to get home."

Mary calls to them again, one hand guiding her cart, the other holding something bright green high above her head. It flutters in the breeze, and Terry can't tell what it is.

Hilda points to Mary. "We should see what she wants."

"Hilda, please."

Mary is practically running now. "Look what I found." Terry can't help staring at the woman, her broad victorious smile, the bright green thing she's waving like some bizarre Olympian pennant.

Terry tugs again at Hilda's arm but she won't budge.

Mary pulls the cart up beside them, and the breeze carries the woman's awful smell, like the stench of something dying. Terry imagines the woman decaying before their eyes, a wicked Witch of the West.

"For you," Mary says to Terry, holding in both hands what the girl sees now is a feather boa, richly green, with long, wide plumes—clearly something that was once luxurious, something she would have prized had she found it in Hilda's attic.

"How lovely," Hilda says.

As Mary brings it closer, Terry jumps away with a yelp.

"No, no, it's for you," Mary tells her, closing the space between them, raising the boa higher so she can drape it around the girl's neck.

"Get away from me," Terry screams, shoving Mary with such force the woman loses her balance, tumbles to the ground in a kind of slow-motion pirouette, the boa twisting around her body. "Oh, my god. I'm sorry," Terry says. The urge to reach out and help the woman is strong, but she can't bring herself to touch her.

Hilda lets out a soft moan and bends over Mary, asking if she's okay. The answer is incoherent, but Terry hears no anger in it. She takes a deep breath and holds it, bracing herself for the odor, and offers the woman her hand. The skin feels like parchment, like there's nothing beneath it but dry sand. Mary gets to her feet, reaches for her cart to steady herself. She seems disoriented. "I'm sorry," Terry tells her again. "Are you okay?"

Mary nods, bends to pick up the boa. She offers it once again to Terry, who refuses it more gently this time. The lines around the woman's mouth deepen as she purses her lips and Terry expects her to say something nasty, but she doesn't. "Okay then," Mary whispers, tucking the boa into her cart, and heads back in the direction of the Goodwill bin.

"Goodbye," Hilda calls, but Mary doesn't turn around. Hilda's eyes stay fixed on the woman, whose gait seems labored now, and Terry wonders if she's really all right.

"I hope she's okay," Terry says.

Hilda's face is blotchy, her eyes watery. "I haven't seen Carol in so long," she says. "I was sure she'd never speak to me again."

"Her name is Mary."

Hilda responds in a way that frightens Terry, waving her away as if the facts are as plain as day. She goes on talking about Carol, a friend she thought had moved away—a misunderstanding that pulled them apart, bits and pieces that don't add up. "She was a year ahead of me in school."

"But that's not Carol," Terry insists. "That's Mary." She wants her to stop this. "She lives in Brentwood, where the DuPont plant used to be."

"Of course, it's Carol. She worked at the skating rink on the weekends."

Terry lets the chairs slide down her arm. "That's Mary. Do you understand me? Mary." She wants Hilda to be present, to be here with her.

Hilda turns to look at her, perhaps remembering where she is. "Not Carol?"

"No. It's Mary."

Hilda's tears come suddenly, freely, as if here and now is a brutal place.

Terry touches Hilda's cheek. "What's wrong?"

Hilda can't seem to find the words for what she wants to say. There's a sigh, barely audible, as if she's resigned to a pain that can't be eased. Terry has seen this many times now, this coming in and out of what's real, back and forth in time, and each retreat, no matter how brief, erodes something Terry has not had the courage to question, not in a serious way. Things end. She's had to face that. But this is different, because there is no one who loves her like Hilda, no world that makes sense without her.

"Grandma, talk to me. Tell me what's wrong. Tell me what I can do."

Hilda takes some tissues out of her bag, dabs her eyes. There was a time, not that long ago, when Terry rarely saw her grandmother cry. Her tissue packets remained in her pocketbook until they came apart and got tossed out. But these tears comfort Terry. Hilda's here with her again. "Everything's going to be all right," Terry says, though she knows that can't be true. Still, she wants Hilda to believe her, to believe what *she* believes, that they'll never be separated.

Terry hears the crack of a bat, the little crowd cheering the runner on. The sound has such energy, such force. She wishes she could see what becomes of it, what difference it will make to the game. The cheers intensify and she imagines Danny reaching home, arms extended in a reckless head-first slide. He's hurt himself more than once that way. Maybe it's the danger itself that makes it worth the try, to risk all without a guarantee, to let the act itself be the reward, to have a single moment that makes whatever follows unimportant. She wonders how that would feel, to revel in uncertainty. She relaxes her grip on the chairs, realizing how tightly she's been holding on. She feels her shoulders sink, her jaw unclench.

As the noise from the game subsides, Mary's voice travels across the parking lot, and Terry looks to see who she's talking to, but, of course, there's no one with her. She's at the bin again, bartering with the universe, holding up a shirt, then a shoe, putting them down, dismissing each one as if its shortcomings are nothing she hadn't expected. The boa is draped regally around her neck.

"She still has the boa," Hilda says.

"Yes, I see it." From this distance, the boa doesn't look to Terry as garish as it did up close, as out of place, and she scolds herself for failing to understand its beauty. It adorns Mary's coat like the perfect accessory, like it's all that's needed to offset her shabby frame. It's a party tog, a mark of celebration, and Mary wears it as if even this ordinary day warrants joy.

"It *would* look good with your jacket."

"I'd be a stand-out," Terry says, finding she's able to laugh, able to see the thing another way, maybe the way Mary does, like a prize untarnished by decay. She fears she won't see Hilda that way once she gets worse. Already there are changes Terry detests. And someday, maybe even soon, Hilda may mistake her for Greta again but for longer than a moment, happy to have her daughter with her, unaware that the granddaughter she once treasured has been displaced. "Do you think she'd still let me have it?"

"Hmmm. I don't know," Hilda says, sounding not the least surprised at Terry's change of heart. Hilda has rarely pointed out her granddaughter's shortcomings, conveying instead a confidence that Terry will come around on her own. Hilda's faith in her has sometimes made Terry feel kinder than she knows herself to be. "Maybe if we offered her some tea?"

"Yes," Terry agrees, glimpsing what's necessary. She'll have to get close to it, all of it—the ratty boa, Mary's smell, the maddening confusion, her grandmother's tears, her mother's bitterness and her own despair—and then hold Hilda's hand again and again, as if for the first time, through each uncertain moment. "Yes," she says, "let's try that. Some tea."

THE SORROW FOR HER LOSS

Robert is upset about the old woman who left Brooklyn to come and live in our guest room while he was away in Boston last week. She sings to herself—old Irish sea chanteys, they sound like—late into the night. She cooks breakfast. This morning it was her plaster-of-paris corn muffins and the black tea she keeps in an old mayonnaise jar on the shelf in the guest room closet. The kids are complaining. Robert wants an explanation. It's complicated.

When I was a sophomore in high school, they called Ellen Tisen out of geometry class to tell her her father had a heart attack. The teacher stepped outside with her. The nurse was out there, the cheerleading coach, her aunt. I envied her.

I was already pretty good by then at making up stories about how my father had died. It was the easiest way to explain why he wasn't around. I never used heart attacks. I went in for slow exits. Sometimes I'd say we were still paying off brain surgeons bills.

My father's real death came three months ago, without fanfare. Not even a break in routine. A call from Maggie, my oldest sister. Something about his liver. He was in his chair, watching the Yankees, cigarette butts spilling over his tray. In his refrigerator they found Budweiser and a jar of something that may once have been relish.

I got the story in two parts because Maggie called on my night to make dinner, and preparations had reached that critical point when delay brings disaster. I considered telling Maggie to hold on while I called Robert into the kitchen to tell him my father died so would he please finish the fettuccini. But I was afraid he wouldn't believe me, assume I was trying to escape dinner duty. When we first met, I told him a whopper about multiple fractures from a head-on collision leaving my father paralyzed on his left side until he died—slow. He'd think I was up to my old tricks. So I told Maggie I'd call her back.

I had no difficulty eating the fettuccini, no lump in my throat, no immediate feelings about the news. The last time I saw my father I was eleven years old. He was sitting alone with his head in his hands on our lumpy, threadbare couch while my mother dragged a beat-up valise and the last of their seven children out the door. Maggie didn't have much more to tell me when I called back. He was still living in Brooklyn; he'd be buried there. I had no intention of attending.

I suppose you might say the reason the old woman is in our guest room is because I had no one to tell about his death. I kept thinking of Ellen Tisen. People were so nice to her when her father finally died. The entire sophomore class chipped in for flowers and a gift to his favorite charity.

Everyone I knew thought my father had died years before. I kept the fantasies to myself. Like the one where I find my dad on my doorstep one morning and he tells me he's been following my life from afar and he's very proud that I got a scholarship and that I became a teacher and that my kids are beautiful and that they've been raised so well. He hopes we can start a new relationship. My father is played by Robert De Niro in this. In another I arrive at some distant cousin's wedding and there he is, waiting for me, this time looking more like Sean Connery. He tells me he's been through a rough time, but he's patented a formula that keeps the head on a beer. He wants me to leave everything and tour the breweries of Germany with him.

Maggie said the wake was well attended. I wasn't surprised. The Irish can't resist mingling with the dead. I pretended I didn't want to hear about it. Of course, she knew it was an act, sent me an email with directions to the gravesite. I never told Robert I was going. It was a long drive on a nasty day, to a nasty part of Brooklyn. Boarded windows, abandoned cars, graffiti in the most unlikely places. The cemetery was one of the few places still open for business. I turned the car into the gate, drove slow, looked for the turns Maggie had described. I came to the place where she said the grave would be, turned off the car, dismissing the thought that it might not start again for me later, that I'd be stranded there. I left the car in the narrow lane. From the looks of things, I wouldn't be in the way of many visitors. Few of the graves were cared for, and weeds had grown past most of the headstones. The wind took gum wrappers and McDonald's Styrofoam into circles, nests of garbage where kids had probably gathered in darkness.

I started for the top of the hill. The day was sunless and getting colder, the ground hard. The weeds pulled at my pant legs. The wind was damp, like when a rain's starting up. It brought a rotting smell from the bay.

I didn't see her until I was at the top of the hill. She was maybe twenty yards below me, right where Maggie said the grave would be. She was looking down, her arms folded across her chest, like she was waiting for an explanation, or her turn on line. She had on a dark raincoat and one of those mesh shopping bags hung from her elbow. I watched her a long time. She was old, had skinny shapeless legs, pepper gray hair that she must have set with pin curls.

I wondered who she was, what she knew. Then her whole body sighed, and she stepped away, down toward the lane on the far side of the cemetery. I walked to the grave, stood where she stood. An arrangement of carnations, dried and brown, had been set aside and lay nearby. The earth of the grave was still darker than the ground around it. The woman had turned up the dirt in the center to plant some mums, or someone had. I got to my knees, touched the dirt. Fresh. The smell of the earth mixed with the sour smell from the bay.

The grave marker bore the dates and his name. Michael Mulvaney. I shivered. Miles from home, in a place as foreign and forbidding as a bad dream, I knelt at the grave of someone who was supposed to be mine, someone irreplaceable. But I had no sense of that, no ache.

Yet, oddly, the flowers stirred something, as if I'd witnessed something private. One person, at least, had cared enough about him to say good-bye, and that made him seem less like a stranger. I wanted more. Not De Niro or Connery. I wanted the real guy, the true story. I had a right to it.

I stood up, expecting to see the old woman—near the gate maybe—but she wasn't there. I felt frantic then, afraid I'd lost the only link to him. I ran to the exit, breathless, almost panicky. I didn't see her anywhere. How could she have walked so fast? I wandered for a block or two, away from the cemetery into the neighborhood's colorless streets. Just ahead five or six boys had staked their claim to the corner, drummed a violent rhythm against the mailbox. I didn't want to pass them so I turned. Onto 45th Street? 46th? I couldn't be sure. The street sign was decapitated. But there she was, the woman with the silly mesh shopping bag, coming out of a grocery store just down the street.

"Hey," I called. "Wait." She stopped, eyed me suspiciously as I rushed across the street toward her.

"You're the one was in the cemetery," she said when I got close. There was a brogue.

"May I talk to you?"

She sized me up with an ungentle glance.

"You knew him?" I said.

"Who?"

"Michael Mulvaney."

"What difference is it to you?" The woman left me there, continued up the street, but I caught up.

"Do you mind if we talk?" I said, but she gave me a side look, kept moving at her own pace as if to say it was no concern of hers whether I talked or not.

"My name is Eileen," I said.

She paused a second, looked at me more carefully this time. "His youngest girl?"

"Yes," I said, but she went silent again. I walked beside her, waited. Several blocks went by, blocks of windowless buildings, children inexplicably joyful in their abandoned Chevies.

The woman seemed to sense my distress at how run down everything was, the storefronts drab and bare, the buildings desperately needing repair. "Don't be thinkin' this wasn't a fine neighborhood at one time," she said.

"Hmmm," I said, as if I understood. We came to her building, a six-story wreck of a place, different from the others only because it was still inhabited. On the stoop were three men and a young woman in a short, tight skirt. We barely had room to pass. As we climbed the steps, I watched the old woman close herself in, eyes down, mesh bag clutched to her skinny chest. The foursome didn't appear to expect a greeting from her. They laughed, exchanged mocking remarks in a singsong Spanish.

"David Braverman once owned this building," she told me when we got inside. We started up the first flight of stairs. "It was taken care of then," she said. Each time we reached a landing, she stopped, looked at the chipping paint or the broken banister and sighed. "The owners don't even collect the rent now." She talked between the long pauses she needed to catch her breath for the next flight. "We send it to a post office box." I heard kids yelling several floors below, then their pounding footsteps gaining on us. She braced herself, gripped the swaying banister, veins swollen on the back of her hand. The kids overtook us in a mad, wild rush of jumps and squeals and leaps and screams. "Jesus, Mary, and Joseph," she said. Not likely.

The next floor was hers. 6B. I saw the tension leave her face as she worked the stubborn locks to get us in. "Come into the kitchen," she said as we entered. I was relieved we wouldn't have to meet under the mournful gaze of Our Lady of the Magnavox mounted on the TV in the living room.

"It wasn't always like this, you know." She pulled aside the frayed lace curtain to survey the damage in the street below. "That was Kaufman's deli, right there. Now all they've got is green bananas. The smell of it. I can't go in. I tell you it breaks my heart. There's nobody left anymore."

She came away from the window, moving more slowly now, looking older than she did in the street, as if it was safe to let some of her defenses down here. She got the kettle, filled it with water, and put it on the stove, then took an old mayonnaise jar down from a yellowing metal cabinet. "We'll be needin' some tea," she said. The tea in the jar was loose and black.

"The jar makes a good canister for your tea?"

"Keeps the roaches out."

I was relieved to hear it.

"You knew my father a long time?"

She spooned the tea. "Where is it you live again?"

Perhaps she hadn't heard me. "Holmdel," I said.

"What part of Jersey is that?"

"Central." I let her finish fussing with the tea. "Did he tell you much about his family?"

"I suppose it's lovely there." She glanced toward her window again, frowned.

"Yes," I said, almost ready to give up on getting an answer. We stayed quiet. The boiling water began to rattle the kettle. I tried again. "Did he talk much about us?"

"Us?"

"His kids."

"Who, Michael?"

"Yes, my father." I managed not to roll my eyes.

"Your father was a good man. He liked a drink. I'll give you that. But he was a good man all the same." She poured the water into a small teapot then wrapped it in a tea cozy and brought it to the table.

"I guess he talked a lot about the past when he drank?"

"We talked. He knew you were living in Jersey."

"He did?"

"I understand it's a mansion of a house you've got."

"Hardly. But we're comfortable."

"More rooms than a boarding house, I heard."

"We have plenty of room."

"Plenty." She settled herself into the chair opposite mine, as if to consider this concept. "In Derry, it was only the Protestants had plenty." A roach slipped out from behind a cabinet mounted just above us. The woman didn't see it. I pretended the same. "And you have guest rooms, no doubt."

"We have a guest room, yes." She poured tea into my cup, but only enough to observe its color. Unsatisfied, she set the teapot back on the trivet. "So he didn't talk much about his family?" I said.

"I know he kept in touch with your brother Peter."

"Really?"

"Your brother Pete. Now, there's a man who knows his mind."

"Did Peter visit him here?"

"And speaks it too."

"Yes," I agreed, remembering the many times we'd locked horns. "So you've met my brother Peter?"

"Met him at the wake. I don't recall seeing *you* though."

"I wasn't there."

"Hmmm," she said, sounding like an unhappy headmistress.

"Did you know my father a long time?"

"Twenty years, give or take," she said curtly. I was sure she was annoyed.

"That's a long time."

"I suppose."

"This isn't bothering you, is it?" I said. "Talking about him?"

"And why would it be botherin' me?"

"I just wondered if he talked much about us. About his children?"

"Your father could talk the collar off a monsignor. He had a way about him." A smile crossed her face, lighting her eyes. "Even with these god-forsaken Puerto Ricans. And them not understandin' a word he said. It was just a way he had, a charm about him."

I watched her test the tea again.

"I remember one time—this was before Braverman sold the building—Dave was making his rounds for the rent and neither of us had it. He liked the rent on time, Braverman. Well, wouldn't you know your father got him to comparing Derek Jeeter to the likes of Mickey Mantle, got him so worked up he forgot what he came for." Satisfied with the tea, she poured it into the cups, this time motioning for me to help myself to sugar and milk.

"But the best was when those holy rollers would come to the door, passin' out their Bible comics. *A moment of your time,* they'd say, and then he'd start, talkin' in tongues like he'd been touched by the Holy Ghost himself." She stirred her tea, looked toward the window, absently, taken by her memories. That bothered me, that place she had that she could go to, a way back to him, back to the answers I wanted.

I put some sugar into the tea and tasted it, expecting something really good after the way she'd fussed over it. And it was. I told her that, wanting to get her attention back.

"I have to go all the way up to the Bronx for it, near Gaelic Park, where my sister lives."

"You have a sister?"

"Catharine," she said, and her tone told me all I needed to know about how well they got along.

"Did you come to America together?"

"No, no. She's only been here ten years. Her boys came over, so she followed. Let's just say she's not adjusting well." She sounded harsh. Clearly this wasn't something she wanted to talk about.

I waited a moment, tried again. "Were we ever on his mind?"

"Family's a complicated business," she said.

Enough already. I wanted to smash the teacup. "Did he know I went to college? That I had two children? What the hell did he tell you about himself?"

"He'd tell me what he was in a mood to tell me"

"He had seven children, you know, sixteen grandchildren. I bet he never knew their names."

She looked directly at me then, puzzled maybe, as if wondering if I was truly as clueless as I seemed. "I'll show you something," she said, then got up. I listened to her steps as she walked to what must have been the last of the railroad rooms, returned with a photograph, placed it down in front of me. It was an old, black-and-white, scalloped-edged photo. Small and square. At least twenty people were crowded onto a couch in an effort to get everyone into the picture.

They were seated on laps, draped across the back of the chair, squeezed together on the floor in front. I didn't recognize anyone at first. Then I looked more closely. On the floor in front of the couch my father was holding my little brother on his lap. My sister Maggie was on one side of him; I was on the other. He had one of my long braids tucked between his nose and his upper lip. I was no more than eight.

I felt a squirrel's urge to put the photo into my bag, hoard it away to study alone, their faces, their clothes. "He gave you this?" I said.

"He kept it in his wallet, wouldn't part with it, even at the end. It was on his night table."

I held it for a long while, and a little of the hardness went out of her look, as if she was tempted to give me a second chance.

"There's more where that came from. With his things."

"You have them, his things?"

"There's not much. They're yours if you want them." I saw that she didn't want to part with them, these odds and ends of somebody else's life, pictures of people who were really my people, not hers. I saw that she loved him.

I slid the photo across the table to her. "Oh, no. That's all right. You keep them. Maybe I could just have a look at them some day."

"You're always welcome here," she said. "Deirdre's my name. He hated it. Called me Clover."

"Clover," I said. It sounded so right for her.

"Or maybe I'll bring them to you some time, to that fine house of yours."

"Yes, that would be nice. You could stay over."

"I wouldn't want to be a bother," she said, then filled my cup with the tea again, as if we'd done this before, as if she knew without asking that I'd want more.

ABOUT THE AUTHOR

Mary Ann McGuigan's short fiction appears in *The Sun,* *Massachusetts Review, North American Review,* and many other journals. Her collection *PIECES* includes stories named for the Pushcart Prize and Best of the Net. Her creative nonfiction can be found in journals such as *Brevity, The Rumpus, X-R-A-Y,* and *The Citron Review.* The Junior Library Guild and the New York Public Library rank Mary Ann's young-adult novels among the best books for teens, and *WHERE YOU BELONG* was a finalist for the National Book Award. You can subscribe to her free monthly newsletter, offering links to many of her published stories and essays, on her website: www.maryannmcguigan.com.

ABOUT THE PRESS

Unsolicited Press is based out of Portland, Oregon and focuses on the works of the unsung and underrepresented. As a womxn-owned, all-volunteer small publisher that doesn't worry about profits as much as championing exceptional literature, we have the privilege of partnering with authors skirting the fringes of the lit world. We've worked with emerging and award-winning authors such as Amy Shimshon-Santo, Brook Bhagat, Elisa Carlsen, Tara Stillions Whitehead, and Anne Leigh Parrish.

Learn more at unsolicitedpress.com. Find us on Instagram, X, Facebook, Pinterest, Bsky, Threads, YouTube, and LinkedIn. Unsolicited Press also writes a snarky newsletter on Substack.